THE
MISSING
SKULL

JOHN WILSON

ORCA BOOK PUBLISHERS

Library and Archives Canada Cataloguing in Publication

Wilson, John (John Alexander), 1951–, author
The missing skull / John Wilson.
(The seven prequels)

Issued in print and electronic formats.
ISBN 978-1-4598-1158-4 (paperback).—ISBN 978-1-4598-1159-1 (pdf).—
ISBN 978-1-4598-1160-7 (epub)

I. Title.
PS8595.I5834M57 2016   jc813'.54   c2016-900487-2
c2016-900488-0

First published in the United States, 2016
Library of Congress Control Number: 2016933637

Summary: In this middle-grade novel, Steve travels to northern Ontario
and ends up looking for the skull of a famous painter.

*Orca Book Publishers is dedicated to preserving the environment and has
printed this book on Forest Stewardship Council® certified paper.*

Orca Book Publishers gratefully acknowledges the support for its publishing
programs provided by the following agencies: the Government of Canada
through the Canada Book Fund and the Canada Council for the Arts,
and the Province of British Columbia through the BC Arts Council
and the Book Publishing Tax Credit.

Design by Teresa Bubela
Cover photography by iStock.com

ORCA BOOK PUBLISHERS
www.orcabook.com

Printed and bound in Canada.

19 18 17 16 • 4 3 2 1

To the memory of Tom Thomson.

ONE

"But they're the best band in the world. Dave Grohl is awesome, and this'll be my only chance to see them." I'm trying to keep my voice calm, but it's tough. If I start to sound whiney, Mom will overreact and I won't have a prayer of going to the Foo Fighters concert. I have to show her how rational and mature I can be.

"I'm sure they'll come back when you're a bit older," Mom says as she begins to unload the dishwasher.

The dishwasher's a good sign. If she's doing something while she talks to me, it means she's not taking it all too seriously, so I have a hope. "The Foo Fighters are famous all around the world," I say slowly. "They tour everywhere. It might be years before they return to Toronto."

"They have an awfully silly name," Mom says, rattling cutlery into the drawer.

Mom's sudden change of direction throws me momentarily, but how dangerous can a band with a silly name be?

Mom turns from pulling dinner plates out of the dishwasher and looks at me. I think I've made it. She's going to say yes, but then her brow furrows. "You're awfully young to be going to a rock concert on your own."

My stomach lurches at Mom's mention of my age. This is the big stumbling block. I throw out all my best arguments at once. "My birthday's coming up. I'll be thirteen by the time of the concert. You could drop me off and pick me up afterward. I'll have my cell with me, so I can call when I get to my seat, at the intermission and at the end. Besides, I won't be going alone. Sam will come with me." This last is stretching the truth a bit. Sam is probably going through exactly the same process as I am right now, but we decided that if we each presented the other as being allowed to go, it would increase our chances.

"Grohl's amazing. He writes most of the band's songs, he's a multi-instrumentalist, and he's played with everybody. Including Paul McCartney," I add, knowing he's Mom's favorite singer. She looks interested, and I feel confident. I should probably shut up at this point, but sometimes my mouth just runs off on its own. "He used to be the drummer with Nirvana."

Mom doesn't know many modern bands—she's more of a Beatles or Rod Stewart sort of fan—but she has heard of Nirvana. "Didn't the singer from that band, something Cocaine, kill himself?"

"Kurt Cobain," I correct softly.

Mom goes quiet and stares at me. I hold my breath. She shakes her head. "You're just a bit too young, Steven. Maybe in a couple of years."

"It's not fair," I say. I'm speaking too loud, but I'm disappointed and angry at having worked hard for nothing. "I never get to do anything. You'd let DJ go to the concert. You let him go to Central America at spring break." I'm standing now, my fists clenched and my anger building as much at my perfect brother as at Mom. "DJ gets to do anything he wants."

"That's not fair, Steven." Mom's standing by the open dishwasher door, a sparkling casserole dish in her hand. "You know DJ wasn't on his own. Your grandfather took him for a treat."

"It was *almost* like being on his own." I say it bitterly, though secretly I'm disappointed that I haven't been taken anywhere yet. "If anything had gone wrong, what could Grandfather have done? He's old."

I turn and storm off to my room. Mom calls my name, but I ignore her. I try to slam my door dramatically, but the effect is spoiled by the pile of T-shirts and jeans spilling out into the hallway. I kick them out of the way, push the door shut and collapse onto my bed. Before I even have a chance to feel sorry for myself, the door opens and my annoying twin brother, DJ, pokes his head inside. "You and Mom having a fight?" he asks.

"Noooo," I say.

"It's about that dumb concert you and that nerdy kid Sam want to go to, isn't it?"

"Sam's not nerdy just because he's into Warhammer."

"So it's not nerdy to spend your life on your own, painting monsters and then sitting around a big table with other nerds playing with them?"

I want to defend my friend, but when DJ describes Sam's hobby that way, it does sound nerdy. I change the topic. "Foo Fighters are cool. Just because you're into dead guys like Elvis and old wrinkly dudes like the Stones doesn't mean that everybody else is dumb." I emphasize this point by hurling a pair of balled-up socks at DJ.

He ducks out the door, but a moment later his head reappears. "Elvis is the King," he says and closes the door before I can find something else to throw at him.

I drag out my phone and call Sam. He answers right way. "Any luck?" I ask.

"Nah," Sam says. "Mom says I'm too young to go on my own."

"Same here," I say.

"I even suggested that Dad come with us so we wouldn't be on our own, but he said he would rather have his teeth pulled out without anesthetic."

"That sucks."

"Yeah. Still, maybe there'll be a big game night on the same day, so I'll go to that instead. You should take up gaming, Steve. Warhammer's sooo cool."

"I'll think about it, Sam. Talk to you soon."

I hang up and sit, thinking. I'm annoyed at not being allowed to go to the Foo Fighters concert, but I knew it was a long shot. What's really bothering me is DJ.

At spring break, Grandfather took him to Central America for a holiday. It isn't that I want to hang out for a week with my grandfather. Sure, he did some cool stuff when he was young, but he's an old guy now, and I can't see him and me wanting to do the same thing on holiday. It's DJ who bugs me. He's been unbearable in the months since he came back, saying what a wonderful time he had but refusing to give me any details. He won't even tell me what country he went to, saying that I'd just blabber about it to Mom, and he doesn't want her worrying about the cool stuff he did—like he discovered pirate treasure or something. Still, he *did* go somewhere, and anywhere in Central America has to have been better than what I'm doing, which is hanging out all summer in Toronto, with only my paper route and Sam for excitement.

When Grandfather took DJ, he said my turn would come because he planned to take all six of his grandsons on a special trip when we were around twelve or thirteen. It's almost time to go back to school, and he hasn't said another word about it. I drag over my laptop and pull up a

Foo Fighters video on YouTube. At least it'll distract me from thinking that I might have to spend the night of the concert gaming with Sam and his nerdy buddies.

TWO

When the doorbell rings, I don't get up to answer it. I know it's Grandfather showing up for lunch, and Mom will get to the door first anyway. Then they'll sit and talk about family for half an hour. Mom will call me when lunch is ready. So the knock on my door comes as a surprise.

The door opens and Grandfather steps in. He's wearing a dark suit and red tie, as if lunch with Mom, DJ and me is some sort of big deal, and he's holding a padded envelope under one arm. His hair is white, neatly brushed, and when he smiles at me, the wrinkles that cover his face deepen even more. Grandfather's in his eighties, but he keeps himself in shape and doesn't even use a cane. His mind is sharp, and he can easily beat us all at Scrabble and Cranium. He claims it's because he's spent his life doing crossword puzzles. He's the oldest person I know, but when I look in his eyes, there's a sparkle that says he doesn't feel that way inside.

"Hi, Steve," he says. "Well, you've finally got your room exactly the way you like it," he adds, glancing around at the mess on my floor that Mom is always trying to get me to clean up.

I'm about to say something about this being my space so I can keep it any way I like, but he sits on the end of my bed, hands me the envelope and says, "I've brought you a present."

"Thank you," I say as I tear the end off the envelope. An old hardcover book falls onto my bed. It has a brightly colored cover and is by Rex Stout, a guy I've never heard of.

"It's *Fer-de-Lance*, the first Nero Wolfe mystery," Grandfather explains. I guess it's obvious from my face that I have no idea what he's talking about, so he continues. "Nero Wolfe was a hero of mine when I was your age. My parents gave me this book for my birthday when it was first published in 1934, and I read every title after that, thirty-three in total, until the last one in 1975. I know you like mysteries, so I thought you might enjoy this one."

"Thanks," I say again. I'm slightly disappointed that Grandfather's given me this big old hardcover book. A paperback or even an ebook would have been more convenient, but he probably thinks he's giving me something special since it was his so many years ago. "What does *Fer-de-Lance* mean?"

"It's the name of a highly poisonous snake. I know it's not a very modern present, but I wanted to give you something that was precious to me and that will fill your spare time when we go on our road trip."

"Road trip?"

"Sure. Remember I told you that I was going to take each of my six favorite grandsons on a special trip?"

I nod. "But you only have six grandsons."

"Then that just proves you must be my favorites. Anyway, DJ's the oldest, so he had his trip at spring break and now it's your turn."

"DJ's only fifteen minutes older than me," I say, vaguely annoyed about Grandfather's buying into DJ's claim to be the older brother even though we're twins. "And DJ got to fly to Central America," I say, unable to hide my disappointment that all I get is a road trip.

"True," Grandfather says, "but I can't give each of you the same adventure. Besides, there are no airports where we're going."

"Where are we going?" A spark of interest flickers in me.

"I can't tell you."

"Why not?"

"It wouldn't be a mystery then, would it?"

"I suppose not," I say, feeling drawn in despite myself. "When are we leaving?"

"How does tomorrow sound?"

"Tomorrow?"

"No time like the present."

"How long will we be gone?" I ask.

"A few days, maybe a week. And before you ask, I've already cleared it with your mother. Did you have any important plans?"

"I was going to hang out with Sam. We were planning on getting tickets to a concert next month, but Mom says we're too young to go to it."

"What's the concert? I doubt it's the Toronto Symphony at Roy Thomson Hall?"

"No," I say, again not quite sure what he's talking about. "It's the Foo Fighters at the Molson Canadian Amphitheatre." I expect to get the puzzled reaction I get from most adults when I mention the Foo Fighters, but Grandfather surprises me.

"Interesting," he says. "A rock band named after what pilots in the Second World War called unidentified flying objects."

13

"How do you know that?" I blurt out before I remember that Grandfather was a pilot in World War II.

"I know lots of things," he says with a smile. "But lunch will be ready in five minutes. I'll go and see if I can help set the table."

"Okay," I say as he stands and tries to find a clear path to my door. As he closes the door, he adds, "Don't forget to pack the book. It'll be a good opportunity to discover Nero Wolfe."

Okay, on the one hand, I'm getting my trip, but on the other, do I really want a week with just Grandfather somewhere within driving distance of Toronto? He's done some cool stuff and he can tell a good story, but a week of stories? It's not like he'll be able to play soccer with me or hike anywhere—he'd probably fall and break a hip or something. I can see boredom looming.

I decide to give Sam a quick call. "Grandfather just arrived for lunch," I say before Sam can launch into his latest Warhammer adventure.

"He brought me a book," I add, knowing that Sam is the only person I know who reads more than I do.

"Cool. What's it called?"

"*Fer-de-Lance*," I say, checking the cover. "It's by a guy called Rex Stout. He wrote about a detective—"

"Nero Wolfe," Sam interrupts. "He's this brilliant guy who's so fat he never leaves his apartment, but he solves every crime he's told about. He's a genius, like Sherlock Holmes. In fact, there might be a connection. Did you notice that Nero Wolfe and Sherlock Holmes use the same vowels in the same order?"

"Oddly, Sam, I didn't notice that, but I'm really glad I have a friend like you who can point these things out."

"Thanks," Sam says, my sarcasm totally lost on him. "Rex Stout wrote thirty-three Nero Wolfe novels. He's been called the best mystery writer of the twentieth century. He lived in—"

"You're getting this off Wikipedia?" I ask.

Again Sam's nerdy chuckle. "Of course. I'm not old enough to have collected every piece of interesting information in my brain."

"It might be interesting," I say, "but Grandfather could have bought me a new copy. He got this one for his birthday in 1934."

"Wow, that is old."

"Anyway," I go on hurriedly before Sam can launch into some other piece of useless information, "we can't hang out tomorrow. He's taking me on a trip."

"Cool. Central America, like DJ?"

"No, it's a road trip."

"Where to?"

"I don't know. It's a mystery."

Sam's silent for a moment. Then he says, "A mysterious road trip. Maybe he's taking you to Port Hope. I hear it's lovely at this time of year. My grandmother lives there—perhaps you could introduce them."

"Seriously, Sam? You're asking me to introduce my grandfather to your crazy grandmother?"

"Why not? It could be the romance of the century."

"Do you want my reasons in alphabetical order or just as they come to me?"

"Steve! Lunch is on the table," Mom calls from the kitchen.

"Be right there," I shout back. Then to Sam, "I gotta go for lunch. I'll call when I know what exciting place I'll be this week. Have fun in your Warhammer world."

"I will," Sam says. "I'm almost done painting the Chaos War Mammoth. It's awesome. I'll show it to you when you come back. Something to look forward to while your grandfather's dating my grandmother in Port Hope."

"Now you're getting creepy."

"It's one of my specialties. Don't forget to take clean underwear."

"Goodbye, Sam," I say as I hang up.

THREE

"This is the way to the cottage," I say as I look up. We've been driving for about an hour and have almost reached Barrie. Another hour north will take us to Port Carling—what passes for civilization near Grandfather's cottage. "We come up here every year. This isn't a mystery." We're in Grandfather's old Jeep Cherokee, and I've been busy playing tunes on my iPod and messing around on my laptop.

"The mystery's past the cottage," Grandfather says. "I just need to stop off there and pick something up. Did you bring the Rex Stout book?"

"Yeah, it's in my bag. Why's it so important?"

"Oh, it's not important. I just thought you'd enjoy it, and I know how fast you can read. I didn't want you to run out of reading material. You up for grabbing some lunch in Port Carling or Bracebridge?" he asks before I have a chance to ask anything else.

"Let's go to the Old Station," I almost yell. "Their pulled-pork sandwiches are awesome."

"Pulled pork at the Old Station it is," Grandfather confirms. "My treat."

I stare through the windshield at the rolling farmland. It's all so familiar. In a few minutes we'll be in Barrie, where we usually stop to pick up supplies for a weekend at the cottage.

I enjoy coming up here, especially in summer when we can go canoeing and swim off the dock. I also like walking on all the nearby trails, imagining that I'm an early explorer or a voyageur or a trapper. It takes a lot of imagination because it's impossible to go far in cottage country without meeting owners out walking their dogs or running, but it gets me away from DJ. It's not that I don't like my brother—I'd do anything for him and he'd do the same for me—it's just that I need a break from his organizing now and then.

In fact, it was DJ who convinced Mom to let me go wandering off on the trails on my own. When I was eight or nine, I was always taking off. I never ran away. I just wanted to see what was behind those trees or over that hill or around the next corner. It drove Mom crazy, and it was DJ who calmed her down and convinced her I'd be okay as long as I stayed on the trails. He even got Grandfather to find me a trail map and teach me how to read it so that I wouldn't get lost.

It's bit strange going up here without DJ and Mom or a selection of the cousins. I daydream through Barrie and well north as the landscape becomes more rugged and we flash past outcrops of broken rock. I must doze off, because I am jerked awake when we turn onto the dirt road to the lake.

"I'll just be a minute," Grandfather says as we pull up to the cottage and he steps out.

I climb out of the Jeep and stretch. The sun is high, and the lake sparkles. A breeze rustles the trees above me and powers a couple of wind-surfers out on the water. I idly kick at a few fallen branches and circle the Jeep a few times. Then I wander down past the cottage toward the dock. As I draw level with the woodpile I hear voices.

"This is going to be more complicated than you think," a woman says. "The plan is good, but if some-thing goes wrong, I'm going to need more help."

My curiosity is piqued when I hear Grandfather's voice. "Do what you need to do. I'll sort it all out, and Carl will be there to help."

I round the woodpile and see Grandfather talking to a woman. He has his back to me, and the woman is facing me. She's dressed in cargo pants and a red blouse, has long fair hair tied in a ponytail and looks surprised when I appear. She recovers quickly, and her face breaks into a broad smile. "Hello," she says.

Grandfather turns. He looks concerned for a moment, but then his face relaxes and he says,

"Sorry I'm taking so long, Steve. This is Sophie. She and her husband, Carl, live here year round, and I pay them to look after the cottage in winter, clear snow and so forth. I'm just making sure that everything is in order in case winter comes early this year."

Sophie says, "Good to meet you, Steve."

"Are you heading down to the dock?" Grandfather asks.

"Yeah, just stretching my legs," I say.

"Don't go far," he says. "I'm almost done here. I just have to grab something from inside and then we can be on our way."

"Okay. Nice to meet you." I nod to Sophie and continue down to the dock. It's one of my favorite spots. I love to sit on the end, surrounded by the lake, listening to the waves lap at my feet and the loons call out on the water. This time I sit and stare back at the cottage. Something is bothering me about what I've just seen.

Grandfather is still in animated conversation with Sophie. A movement at the edge of the trees catches my eye. There's someone there. I can't see him clearly in the shadow of the trees, but I know it's a guy. He's tall and broad across the shoulders. His head looks shaved, and I think I see camouflage pants and a dark shirt. I wonder if it's Sophie's husband, Carl. He turns his back and moves farther into the shadows. Sophie says something to Grandfather and moves off to join the stranger, reinforcing my thought that it must be Carl. The pair move off along the lakeshore. Grandfather waves at me and heads around to the front door.

As I watch the figures disappear through the trees, I remember what's bothering me. Last year there was more snow than usual around Christmas, and we had to postpone a planned winter trip to the cottage. Grandfather came to visit us instead, and Mom asked if the cottage would be okay. Grandfather had said he was sure it would be because Bill always did such a good job of looking after it. Bill, *not* Carl or Sophie.

I walk back up to the cottage and peer in the side window. Grandfather's standing beside the fireplace, staring at the woodpile beside it. I walk around to the front. The door's ajar, so I push it open and walk in. Grandfather spins around, looking startled, but he recovers quickly, stuffing what looks like a small envelope into his jacket pocket. "I think I heard a rat in the woodpile," he explains, speaking rapidly. "I'll have to get Carl to put some poison down. Just give me a minute and we'll be on our way."

"Sure," I say as Grandfather scans the bookshelves on the other side of the fireplace. "What happened to Bill?" I ask.

Grandfather's hand pauses on the way to the bookshelf. "Bill?"

"Wasn't it someone called Bill who looked after the cottage when there was all that snow last winter?"

"Oh, Bill." Grandfather relaxes and pulls a book off the shelf. "He's going down to Arizona this winter, so I had to get Carl and Sophie. That's what I was talking to her about—just making sure they know what to do." He holds up the book, a hardcover that looks as old as the one he gave me. "This is what I was looking for."

I get a quick glimpse of a clenched fist in front of a ruined building. "It's called *Homage to Catalonia*," Grandfather tells me as he lowers the book. "It's written by George Orwell, one of my favorite authors. I read this long ago and thought I'd enjoy rereading it on this trip. It's about some time Orwell spent in a war in Spain back in the 1930s. You might enjoy reading it when you're a bit older. Now, let's hit the road and get some lunch."

Grandfather heads for the door, and I follow. What he said about Bill going south makes sense—lots of snowbirds head to Florida or Arizona for the winter—but I still have questions. Grandfather is behaving oddly. Normally he's incredibly calm, but I've surprised him twice since we got here. Also, what's so interesting about the woodpile, and what's in the envelope in his pocket?

FOUR

After the best pulled-pork sandwiches in Ontario, followed by a dish of Rocky Road ice cream, we drive north for almost two hours. There's plenty to see—trees, trees, rocks, trees, a bit of water, trees, rocks, trees and more trees. Eventually, we turn off the highway and onto a narrow dirt road. On our left I get glimpses of a lake and some really fancy houses. I'm certainly up for staying in one of those places, but we turn onto a rough track so narrow that the bushes brush the sides of the Jeep and the trees form a solid canopy above us.

"This wouldn't even show up on Google Maps," I comment.

"That's right," Grandfather agrees. "We've dropped right off the radar out here."

I don't find this comment comforting but don't get a chance to ask anything more as we bump around a corner and into a small clearing beside a lake. In the middle sits a cabin. Well, calling it a cabin is being polite. The toolshed at Grandfather's cottage is bigger than this place— and in much better shape.

The walls are roughhewn interlocking logs with what looks like dirt stuffed between them. I think the roof's made from wood shingles, but it's hard to be sure through the thick moss. There's a lean-to sheltering a woodpile on one side of the house, and a stone chimney on the other. The chimney's easily the most solid-looking thing about the cabin. It'll probably be here long after the rest of the place has rotted away, which, judging by the sagging front porch, won't be long from now.

"It's old," I say, pointing out the obvious.

"More than a hundred years old," Grandfather says. "It was originally a trapper's cabin. It's been here since before this became a park."

"Park?" I ask.

"We're in Algonquin Park," he tells me. "It's Canada's oldest provincial park. It was established in 1893."

"And we're going to stay in a cabin that's older than that?" I ask, horrified at the thought.

"A chance to live like your ancestors did," Grandfather says, sounding way happier than I am about the prospect. "Don't worry—the park administration took the cabin over as a ranger station and upgraded it. They rent it out."

Probably not for very much, I think. "When was it upgraded, the 1950s?"

Grandfather chuckles and opens the driver's door. "Let's get in and get settled." He scans the sky. "I think there might be a storm brewing. We can get a fire going later and toast some marshmallows."

I sit and watch Grandfather head for the cabin. This isn't what I expected. It's more like a survival course than anything else. Maybe Port Hope would have been better. I flip my phone open to send Sam a text. There are no bars. "No cell phone reception," I say out loud. This is getting positively Dark Ages. I'll catch the Black Death or something—and there's probably not even an indoor toilet. I stare miserably at the cabin. Toasting marshmallows! Does Grandfather think I'm still six? I sigh and get out of the Jeep. It's going to be a long few days.

I walk past the cabin, which looks sturdier close up, and down to the lakeshore. I groan inwardly as I notice an outhouse in the trees. There's no dock, but the clearing slopes gradually into the water, which laps up onto a line of pebbles. An upturned canoe has been dragged into the trees. I can see a couple of islands out on the lake, and the trees of the far shore. The water looks gray and cold and stretches away to my right and left. The sky is dark and threatening in the distance, and the water is choppy away from the shore. Just as I'm thinking that Grandfather was right about a storm coming, I hear the first long roll of thunder echo down the lake. A few large raindrops rustle the foliage around me and splat onto the shore at my feet. Great. Now we'll be trapped in the cabin and not even able to go canoeing or walking. I kick a stone into the water and turn back to the cabin.

I've only taken a couple of steps when a loud crack from the trees over by the outhouse freezes me in place. I think, bear. No, I think, BEAR!!!! and spin around.

It's getting darker by the minute as the thunderheads roll in, so I have only a vague impression of a big dark shape lumbering into the gloom along the shore between the closely packed trees. I don't run to the cabin, but I walk very fast, glancing often over my shoulder.

As soon as I'm safely inside, I blurt out, "There's a bear out there."

"Almost certainly," Grandfather says in an annoyingly calm voice. He's by the fireplace, breaking sticks for kindling.

"It was over by the outhouse. I heard a noise and saw a shape moving away through the trees."

"Are you certain it was a bear? We often see what we expect to see."

I think back. True, I had panicked at the noise, and the first thing I thought was *bear*, but the shadow in the trees had been vague, just a large shape. It could have been a hunched-over man in a big coat. Now I am getting paranoid. If I go on imagining mysterious people lurking in the darkness, I'm not going to have the courage to use the outhouse. "I'm pretty sure it was a bear," I say.

Grandfather nods. "It was probably just curious. There are lots of bears in the park, but if you don't bother them, they won't bother you. You just need to be careful to be tidy and keep all food and garbage out of reach. Attacks are very rare."

Very rare is more than one, so I don't feel encouraged. Grandfather must see the worry on my face, because he stands up and moves over to the rough wooden table beside what passes for a kitchen. "This place is full of history," he says.

I join him. Here come the stories, I think.

"We're on Canoe Lake, where Tom Thomson died in 1917." Grandfather pauses and looks at me expectantly.

"Who's Tom Thomson?" I ask.

"A famous Canadian artist," Grandfather tells me. "You've heard of the Group of Seven?"

I shake my head and Grandfather sighs the way he does when he can't understand how I know so little. "The Group of Seven defined Canadian art in the 1920s and '30s. They traveled all over the country and painted the Canadian landscape like no one else ever had."

"And this Tom Thomson was one of them?" I ask.

"No," Grandfather says. "The group wasn't formed until 1920, and Thomson was dead by then, but he was friends with many of them and influenced their styles. He died under mysterious circumstances while out canoeing on this lake."

"Mysterious circumstances?" I'm being drawn into the story despite myself. Outside, the rain is getting heavier, and the rising wind is rustling the trees.

"He went out fishing in his canoe, and his body was found eight days later."

"So he fell out of his canoe and drowned," I say. "Where's the mystery in that?"

"That was the official story," Grandfather continues, "but if he drowned, why was there no water in his lungs? If he fell out of his canoe, why was there fishing line tied around his legs? Why was his canoe paddle never found either in the canoe or floating nearby? What caused the bruising on the left side of his head?"

Grandfather sits back and smiles at me.

"So what really happened?" I ask as the questions rush around my brain.

Grandfather shrugs. "Accident? Suicide? Murder? Who knows?" He leans forward and stares at me intently. "Perhaps it wasn't a bear you saw by the outhouse."

The windows rattle in a strong gust of wind. It's getting dark in the cabin, and Grandfather's smile is starting to look increasingly creepy.

"What do you mean, not a bear?" I ask. This isn't helping my anticipation of a trip to the outhouse.

Grandfather speaks quietly, forcing me to lean in closer to hear what he's saying. "Some folks hereabouts," he says slowly, "claim they've seen Thomson's ghost." The windows rattle extra loudly, and something bangs against the outside of the cabin, making me jump. "They say the ghost won't rest until the mystery is solved and the person responsible for Tom Thomson's murder is punished."

FIVE

The storm is violent but it's over quickly. While Grandfather brings in wood from the pile outside and builds up the fire, I look around the cabin. It doesn't take long. There's only the main room and two tiny bedrooms at the back, each barely large enough for a single bed, small table and closet.

The main room has a loveseat and a couple of chairs arranged around a low table in front of the fireplace. There's a collection of about a dozen tattered paperback books on the mantel. Opposite, there are four rough chairs around the table, a countertop with a washbasin, assorted plates, a two-burner propane stove and a row of hooks with pots and pans and kitchen utensils hanging from them. Several framed photographs of the lake, some of which look quite old, hang on what open wall space there is. There's also a Google Earth image that shows part of the lakeshore with what I presume is our cabin marked with a red circle. We seem to be right at the beginning of a row of much bigger cabins and empty lots.

When the rain eases, we bring our packs, the cooler and the boxes of food in from the Jeep and heat up some chili. As we wait for supper, Grandfather tidies up, straightening the pictures on the walls, adjusting the dishes, even sorting the dog-eared books on the mantel.

"I like to keep my books tidy," he says over his shoulder. "Alphabetical by author, *a* at the beginning and *z* at the end. That way I always know where to find my favorite authors."

I've always known Grandfather can be annoyingly tidy, but this borders on obsessive—and how many books is he planning to read while we're here? I don't say anything though.

As we eat, Grandfather tells me more about the mystery of Tom Thomson. "Thomson was an experienced canoeist and outdoorsman, so an accident seems unlikely."

"Maybe he killed himself deliberately," I suggest.

"Suicide's a theory, but he left no note, didn't seem unhappy and took supplies of food with him. And how did he get the bruise on his head? Did he hit himself with a rock?"

"If his death wasn't an accident or suicide," I say, mopping up the last of my chili with a piece of bread, "it must have been murder, so who killed him?"

"That's the million-dollar question," Grandfather says. "There were rumors that Tom was engaged to a local girl and that she was pregnant. This would have upset and annoyed her family, but enough to kill Tom?

"Also, the night before he disappeared, Tom apparently had an argument with a local man,

Shannon Fraser. Fraser later said he helped Tom go out the day he died, so he had opportunity. Fraser was an unpleasant man who was disliked by many, including Tom's fiancée and the local park ranger.

"Alternatively, there was a lot of game poaching going on in the park, and poachers might have reacted violently if Tom ran into them. There was also a railway line that ran through the park, carrying soldiers off to the First World War. Sometimes these men deserted, and they wouldn't want to be caught."

"So the murderer was someone in the fiancée's family, the unpleasant Shannon Fraser, a poacher or an army deserter."

"Those are the main suspects," Grandfather agrees.

"It's like the game of Clue," I say with a laugh. "I think it was Unpleasant Fraser in the Parlor with the Poker."

"You might not be too far off the truth," Grandfather says. "One story that's been suggested is that Fraser punched Tom during their argument, and Tom fell and hit his head on the fire grate. Either he died right away and Fraser dumped the body next day, or Tom died the next day from bleeding in the brain."

"That sounds like the most reasonable theory. Have we solved the mystery?"

"Oh no," Grandfather says with a grin. "I doubt if the mystery of how Tom Thomson died can ever be solved now, so long after the event."

I'm about to ask where the fun is in a mystery that can't be solved when he goes on. "There's another mystery, a much more recent one that I was involved in, and that's the mystery I've brought you up here to solve."

It takes me a moment to realize what Grandfather is saying. "You've brought me here to solve a mystery?"

Grandfather's grin broadens. "You didn't think I would bring you all the way up here just to sit by the lake and listen to my old stories, did you?"

"Well…I…" I stammer. "I did kind of wonder why DJ got to go to Central America and I came to Canoe Lake."

"As you know, I plan to take each of you grandsons on a trip. You're all very different, even twins like you and DJ."

"And brothers like Spencer and Bunny," I add.

"Exactly," Grandfather says with a laugh. "I'm going to have to think about the trip for those two. I want to make each of your trips different, so I've given some thought to each of you. You've always loved mystery stories, Encyclopedia Brown, the Hardy Boys and so on, so I thought I'd give you a real-life mystery to solve. Kind of like a game of Clue in the real world."

"Cool," I say. Suddenly I'm thrilled. This week is looking up. "What mystery are we going to solve?"

"*We're* not going to solve any mystery—*you* are going to solve this on your own. I'll give you the background and a few clues, and the rest will be up to you. You'll have to do some things that might seem odd at the time, and it won't be easy, but you won't have to do anything dangerous, and I'll be looking out for you all the time. Are you up for it?"

I don't have to think long. This is my chance to be a real live detective, to live out one of the novels I love so much. "Sure," I say. "Steve McLean the Super Sleuth at your service. What do I have to do?"

"You have to find Tom Thomson's head."

I guess I look shocked, because Grandfather bursts out laughing. "Not literally. What you have to do is work out where his skull is."

"It's not with his body?"

Grandfather shrugs. "Let me give you a little background, but first we'll need a bit of light."

I look around and see that it is getting gloomy in the cabin. The flickering firelight doesn't show much beyond the hearth. Grandfather removes our dishes, throws a couple of logs on the fire and lights two oil lanterns. One lantern he hangs from a hook on one of the ceiling beams, the other he places between us on the rough table.

"A number of years back," Grandfather begins as he settles into his chair, "I came up here on business and fell in love with the landscape. My business ended earlier than expected, and it was a beautiful day, so I rented a canoe to explore the islands you saw offshore. On the largest one I met an old fisherman, Jim Davis, who was building a fire to brew some tea. He invited me to join him, and we fell to talking. Since we were on Canoe Lake and drinking tea a matter of meters from where Thomson's body was found, the conversation turned to the artist's mysterious death."

I'm leaning forward, totally riveted by Grandfather's tale of mystery and murder. I can hear the hiss of the lantern and feel its heat on my cheeks.

"Jim couldn't cast any light on Thomson's death, but he had some interesting things to say about what happened after. When they found it, Thomson's body had been in the water for eight days. I'm sure you can imagine it wasn't in very good shape, so they buried it quickly in the cemetery at Mowat. When Thomson's family in Leith, just outside Owen Sound, were told of the tragedy, they asked for the body to be sent home so he could be buried in the family plot. This was done in a sealed casket, and a funeral service was held. Shortly after, a tale spread that the undertaker had been too lazy to dig up Thomson's body and had sent an empty sealed casket to Leith."

"So Thomson's grave is empty?" I ask.

"Well, he has two graves. One of them has to be empty. In 1956 Judge William Little and three friends decided to find out which one. One morning in September they started digging around in Mowat Cemetery. The problem was, no one had bothered or had time to put up a tombstone back in 1917, so the exact site of the first grave had been lost."

"In daylight? Didn't any of the townspeople notice four guys digging holes in the town cemetery?"

"You would think," Grandfather says with a sly grin. "But we're in Mowat right now. Did you see many people around when we drove in?"

I shake my head.

"Used to be," Grandfather goes on. "Once upon a time there were more than five hundred people living here. The town had a store, lodge, hospital, lumber mill, railway, school—everything a thriving little community needed. But not anymore. The mill and the railway closed, the lodge burned down, and people drifted away. Now there are just a few cabins on the lakeshore. Mowat's a ghost town, and it was when Judge Little did his digging."

"What did they find?" I ask eagerly.

"It took them several attempts, but eventually a spade hit the edge of a wooden box—they'd found a rotting oak coffin."

Nothing could drag me away from the table now.

"One of the men stuck his hand in the coffin and pulled out a bone."

"Ew!" I exclaim at the thought of someone putting their hand in a coffin.

"It was an old coffin, and they were just bones. Remember, these guys were used to hunting and so on. Anyway, they found a complete skeleton and took some bones out to show to a doctor friend they knew."

"Was Jim one of the men?" I ask, thinking I should find out as much as possible if I am going to solve this mystery.

"No," Grandfather says, "but he told me he had Tom Thomson's skull in his garden shed."

SIX

"This guy kept a human skull in his shed? That's sick," I say. When I get over my shock, I remember that detectives need to keep asking questions. "Did you see it?"

"Good question," Grandfather says. "The short answer's no, but let me finish the first part of my story. After the skull and bones were removed in 1956, they were sent to Toronto for analysis. Scientists there determined that the bones belonged to a young First Nations man, about five foot eight inches tall. Since Thomson wasn't of First Nations descent, was over six feet tall and was thirty-nine years old when he died, they concluded it wasn't Thomson's skeleton and sent the bones back for reburial."

I'm disappointed. Every time Grandfather seems to be getting deep into the mystery, he provides an answer. "So Thomson's body *was* moved to Leith," I say.

"A good detective never rushes to conclusions," Grandfather says with a wink. "There's more. There was no *CSI* or *Bones* back in 1956. The skull was determined to be First Nations based on the teeth, a very uncertain way to do things. Same thing with guessing height and age from bones—it's not exact, and we don't know precisely how tall Thomson was. The other interesting thing about the skull was that it had a round hole on the left side."

"Was the hole where the bruise had been seen when the body was found?" I ask excitedly, remembering Grandfather's description of the body from 1917.

"An excellent question that any good detective would ask," Grandfather says.

"How did the Toronto scientists explain the hole in the skull, and how did Jim get the skull?" I blurt out, thrilled that I'm doing so well.

"One question at a time," Grandfather cautions with a smile. "Yes, the hole in the skull was on the left temple, exactly where the bruising had been seen. The scientist who examined the skull claimed that the hole was the result of a surgical procedure called trepanning, where a hole is drilled in the skull to relieve pressure. Trepanning is a very rare procedure and is very unlikely to have been carried out on a young First Nations man in the wilds of Algonquin Park 100 years ago.

"Jim Davis became involved because he was given the job of reburying the bones when they came back from Toronto. He buried most of them, but he stole the skull."

"Why did he steal the skull?"

"Partly because he still believed it belonged to Tom Thomson and partly just for a souvenir."

"Some souvenir. Why didn't you get to see it?"

"You've certainly got a detective's talent for asking questions," Grandfather says with a chuckle. "When I met Jim on the island, he wasn't planning on heading back to his cabin for a couple of days. I couldn't wait that long, so I arranged to return when I had a few days free. Things got a little crazy when I got back to the city, so it was almost a month before I headed back up here. By then it was too late."

"Too late?"

"Jim was dead."

A shiver runs down my spine. "How did he die?"

"His cabin caught fire. No one knows how. Could have been a faulty oil lamp, a spark from the open fire, a fallen cigarette."

"Did the shed burn down as well?"

"Good for you," Grandfather says. "You get straight to the important point. No, the shed wasn't touched."

"So the skull was still in it?"

"That's the strange thing. I went to have a look. The shed was cluttered, but it looked as if stuff had been moved recently, and there was no sign of a skull."

"What happened to it?"

Grandfather says nothing. He simply sits and smiles at me over the flickering lantern.

"That's the mystery?" I guess. "That's what I have to find out?"

"That's the beginning of it."

"Don't I get any other clues?" I ask, not even knowing where I should start without something else.

"You'll get clues as you go along."

"How will I find them?"

"That is the first thing you have to discover." Grandfather stands up. "Now, I think it's time for bed. You have a busy time ahead of you. Perhaps you should introduce yourself to Nero Wolfe. I always find that a few pages of a good story in the evening helps me sleep."

* * *

I unpack my few clothes in my tiny room and carefully place the Rex Stout book on the shelf at the head of the bunk. I have a small battery-powered lamp that doesn't give much light but is enough to read by. I undress, crawl into my sleeping bag and lie there, thinking.

The day has been much more interesting than I had expected. Grandfather acted a bit strangely at his cabin, but lunch was good. The encounter with the possible bear was exciting, and I am getting over my horror at the cabin's primitive-ness. And now I have a mystery to solve. It isn't a real mystery—Grandfather has set it up and will be looking out for me and will help if I get stuck, but I'm excited at the idea. This is going to be a better game than Sam's monster battles on a table.

My mind turns to my first problem—the clues and where to find them. Since I have no idea where to start, I guess that the first clue must be hidden somewhere in the cabin. I promise myself I'll look for it first thing in the morning.

I yawn. How come sitting in a car all day, doing nothing, can be so tiring? I reach up for *Fer-de-Lance*. A few pages will be good before I go to sleep. I prop myself up against the cabin wall and begin reading.

The book is a pleasant surprise. It's a bit old-fashioned, but it's an easy read and I find myself being drawn into Nero Wolfe's world and the crimes he is a genius at solving. After twenty pages I find my eyelids drooping, but I force myself to finish chapter 2.

At first I think the small square of paper at the beginning of chapter 3 is an old bookmark, but then I see the writing on it. *Begin at the beginning. The third along. Check the empty space at the front.*

I turn the paper over, but there's nothing else. Someone has obviously written a note as a reminder, but it might have been seventy years ago. I place *Fer-de-Lance* back on the shelf. Then it strikes me. I'm supposed to find clues, and here's a cryptic note in the book Grandfather has given me and made sure I brought with me.

I'm excited and pleased that I have discovered the first clue but totally confused as to what it can mean. *Begin at the beginning* is simple enough, but the beginning of what—Thomson's death, his burial, his body being dug up years later? And what, or where, is *the third along*? I suppose if I work those out, the *empty space* will make sense.

I puzzle over the clue for a while, but I'm too tired to think straight. I tuck the piece of paper on the shelf with the book and curl up in the sleeping bag. The bunk is surprisingly comfortable, and I only have time to think that this week might turn out to be fun after all before I fall asleep.

SEVEN

I wake up late to the sun streaming through the tiny window of my room, stretch, drag on a pair of board shorts and a Foo Fighters T-shirt and go though to the main room. The door to Grandfather's bedroom is open, so he must already be up. I head outside. The journey to the outhouse is much happier in bright sunlight than in the dark with thoughts of bears running wildly through my head. There's no sign of Grandfather, but the Jeep's here, so I assume he must have gone for a walk. I head back in and dig out some cereal and orange juice.

As I eat, I try to work out the meaning of the first clue. I'm not having much luck until I notice the satellite image from Google Earth pinned to the wall beside the door. I go over and peer at it. The red-circled cabin is definitely ours. I can even see the outhouse and sagging porch. I also notice something I missed the last time I looked—each of the lots along the lakeshore is numbered. Ours in number one, because to one side of us there's nothing but trees. On the other side is cabin two. It's much bigger, fancier and newer than ours, and I can't help feeling a pang of regret that Grandfather didn't reserve something like that for us. The next one along, number three, is just an empty lot—there's no cabin. Number four is another fancy cabin but much smaller than our neighbor. Number five—my eyes swing back. Number three doesn't have a cabin on it. It's an empty lot. An empty space.

I feel a surge of excitement. Our cabin is at the beginning of the row, and the third along the row is empty. Have I solved the first clue?

Didn't Grandfather say he met Jim the fisherman on an island? What if it was one of the islands I saw from the beach and Jim had a cabin nearby—a cabin that burned down, leaving the lot empty? That would make it the beginning of Grandfather's involvement with the missing skull.

It's worth checking out. I scrawl *Gone clue hunting* on a scrap of paper and set it on the table. I consider a sweatshirt, but it's already warm outside, so I slip on my runners and set off. At first I try to head straight through the trees, but the fancy cabin next door is surrounded by a wire fence taller than I am. There's a gate in it, but it's firmly locked. I peer through and see a wide deck above an immaculate lawn that stretches down to the water line, where an impressive dock juts out into the lake. There's a red aluminum boat tied at the end of the dock. I walk along the fence until I get onto the dirt road that runs parallel to the shore.

From the road, our neighbor's is even grander. The wire fence gives way to a high stone wall that's only broken by an imposing wrought-iron gate. I can see a curving drive leading up to a carved front door surrounded by tall pillars that make the place look like an ancient Greek temple. A gold-lettered sign by the gate announces *Shore Mansion Resort Wellness Retreat. Your Destination for Relaxing in Style.* Oddly, the sign has no phone number to call if you happen to be rich enough to afford to stay here. I suppose they don't want just anyone to call.

Lot three is totally different, completely overgrown with willows and dense underbrush. There's no obvious path, so I push my way through as best I can. As I get closer to the lakeshore, the undergrowth thins and I find myself in a clearing. At the widest point, there's a low mound, covered in a tangle of prickly gooseberries. Beside it is a pile of old timber that looks as if it might once have been a building.

As I approach the mound, I see the ends of blackened logs sticking out. Could this be the remains of Jim's burned cabin? If it is, then the pile of timber must be the collapsed remains of his shed.

"What you doing here?" The voice makes me jump. I spin around to see a figure stepping out of the trees.

"N...nothing," I stammer. "I'm staying along the shore and I was just exploring."

"Shouldn't go exploring on other people's property without permission," the man says, stepping forward. He's big, well over six feet tall and broad across the shoulders. His head is shaved, and he has a long black beard. He's wearing camouflage pants and a plaid shirt, and his nose is bent to one side, making his face look off-center. He's frowning at me, and I have a strong urge to run. "This is private land."

"It can't be," I blurt out. "This is a provincial park."

The man looks momentarily uncertain, but he soon recovers. "Some of this land's been owned since before the park came. You wouldn't go wandering around the fancy place next door without an invite, would you?"

"No," I admit. I decide I've got nothing to lose by getting straight to the point. "Did this used to be Jim Davis's place?"

"What makes you think that?" the man asks, tilting his head and peering at me.

"Someone I know met him once and told me Davis had a cabin around here that burned down." I look over at the pile of rubble.

The big man glances over as well. "So what?" he says.

"Nothing, really," I say. I don't want to tell this guy about the mystery I have to solve. "I was just wandering around and got curious."

"Curiosity can get you into trouble," the man says.

"Sorry," I say and turn to leave.

"You're right," the man says. I turn back. "This was Jim Davis's place. He lived here all his life. That was his favorite spot." The man points over to the island close to the shore. "That rocky point at the end of the island. Jim used to sit there for hours, drinking tea, cooking fish and just watching the water. Maybe your grandfather will let you canoe over and take a look."

"Perhaps," I say. "I'll ask him. Thank you."

The man nods and wanders off toward the trees.

I push my way through the undergrowth and to the road. I'm halfway back to the cabin when it strikes me—the man suggested that Grandfather might let me go over to the island, but how did he know I'm here with Grandfather? I'm certain I didn't mention that.

I stop and stare into the trees. A light breeze is rustling the leaves as things begin to fall into place in my head. It's strange that the guy showed up as soon as I got to the clearing where Davis's cabin used to be. It was almost as if he was waiting for me. He was aggressive to begin with but then volunteered the information about Davis's favorite spot on the island. Had the guy just given me the second clue—or advice on how to get the clue? Was this all a setup by Grandfather? My first impression of the guy in the clearing was that he was familiar, but I didn't recognize his face. Was it Carl from Grandfather's cabin? I had seen him, but only as a figure in the trees. If Grandfather was setting up a game of real-life Clue, might he be using people to create the story? It was the sort of thing he would do, and it would explain his conversation with Sophie that I had stumbled upon.

Feeling sure I have cracked a piece of the puzzle Grandfather has given me and excited to take the next step, I run the rest of the way to the cabin.

EIGHT

"Grandfather!" I shout as I burst through the cabin door. I'm met by a wall of silence. The place is exactly as I left it. Grandfather isn't back from his walk yet.

I grab a couple of chocolate-chip cookies from the kitchen and head down to the lake to wait. I eat the cookies and toss stones in the water. It's tough—I'm desperate to tell Grandfather that I've worked out the first clue and am ready to move on to the next stage, but he's off wandering around somewhere.

I stare over at the nearby island. Like the rest of the park, it's tree covered, but a rocky point juts out into the lake. At the end of the promontory, a single pine tree clings to the rock. It's small and twisted and bent back as if struggling to rejoin its companions on the island. I wish Grandfather would return so we could canoe over to the island. Then I think back to what Carl (or whoever he was) said in the clearing. He said that maybe Grandfather would *let* me canoe over to the island, not *take* me over. If Grandfather is setting this whole thing up, maybe he's deliberately staying away to force me to do things on my own. He said as much when he told me why he brought me up here. He said I would have to do some strange things but that he would be looking out for me. Now I know that Carl will be looking out for me as well.

It's not far over to the island, and I've done a fair amount of canoeing at Grandfather's cottage. There's no wind, and the water's calm. I doubt there are strong currents in Canoe Lake. I scan the sky. It's clear, and there's no sign of a storm coming in. I make my decision, jump up and hurry to the overturned canoe in the trees.

The canoe's not very fancy, but it's light and has two paddles and two life vests stored under it. I put on one of the vests and drag the canoe down to the shore and into the water. Before I step in, I make one final check of the lake. It's smooth and flat, like a mirror, but the thought that somewhere just out there something terrible happened to Tom Thomson, and his body wasn't found for eight days, sends a shudder down my spine. But I've made up my mind. I push the thought away, step into the canoe and propel it away from the shore.

At first the paddling is awkward. I'm used to having someone else paddling at the front of the canoe, so the boat seems light and the prow swings from side to side with each stroke. After a while I settle into a rhythm, and the canoe carves more cleanly through the water.

I feel wonderful. Here I am on my own, without DJ telling me what I should be doing, and well on my way to solving the mystery Grandfather has set me. I love the warm air brushing my cheeks as I move forward and the sound of the water lapping against the side of the canoe as I paddle. I let my eyes slide over the tree-covered island and along the rocky shore. I can see why an artist would love to come here to paint: it's beautiful and peaceful.

There's nowhere to land on the rocky point, so I paddle along the shore until I find a spot where I can clamber onto the rocks. There's a rope attached to the bow of the canoe, which I tie to a jutting piece of rock.

The trees on the island are close together and the underbrush is dense, so I scramble along the narrow, rocky strip between the trees and the water. Apart from the lone tree, the point is barren, but there's an open, flat, triangular mossy area between the trees and the rocks of the point. Circles of blackened stones show where people have built fires. I wonder if this is where Jim Davis used to cook his fish and where he told Grandfather the story about Tom Thomson's skull.

I wander around, but I can't see anything that could be another clue. I work my way over the rocks to the lone tree, hoping to find a note pinned to the trunk, but there's nothing, just an old plastic bottle wedged between two rocks. It annoys me that people can be so thoughtless and just throw their garbage away in such a beautiful spot. I check out the bottle in case it's the next clue, but unless there's a coded message in *Coca-Cola Classic*, it's not.

I move back to the mossy area and look around. I'm disappointed. I'd gotten cocky after I discovered the first clue and thought the mystery would be easy to solve. I'd figured there would be an obvious clue here pointing me toward the next one and so on, but there's nothing. I kick at the old fire pits but only succeed in getting my runners dirty. I hear birds calling in the trees and get the feeling they're mocking my failure. In the distance an outboard motor roars—the inhabitants of a holiday cabin, setting out to enjoy the day. Then I notice the path. It's not much more than an animal trail, but it runs off through the trees toward the center of the island. Maybe I'm supposed to follow it. I certainly don't have any other options besides paddling back to the cabin.

I head down the path. In places I have to duck down below branches, and soon my feet and clothes are soaked from walking through the wet grass and brushing against the leaves. I'm about to turn back when the path widens into a clearing. There's nothing in it, but a wider path leads off to my right. I figure it probably leads back to the shore and my canoe, so I head in that direction.

As I turn, I hear a rustling noise off to my left. I spin around but can see nothing between the trees. Inevitably, I think, bear. Hurrying down the path, I make as much noise as possible, whistling and singing what I can remember of the Foo Fighters' latest album.

I can see the shore through the thinning trees and am beginning to relax when someone grabs me from behind, pinning my arms to my sides.

NINE

"Don't do anything silly," a voice I recognize from the ruined cabin says.

My heart rate slows down. This is all a setup. It was dumb of me to think that all of Grandfather's clues would be the same or as easy as the first one. My admiration for Grandfather's plan is growing all the time. "Carl?" I say.

"Who's Carl?"

"Of course, you have to say that," I tell him. "Okay, where do we go now?"

The grip on my arms relaxes. "Down to the shore." Carl transfers his grip to only my left arm and moves beside me. I turn and give him a smile. I get a frosty stare in return. This guy's either miserable in real life or he went to acting classes.

Carl leads me along the last stretch of trail to the shore, where the red aluminum boat that I saw at the resort beside our cabin is tied to a fallen tree. "In," Carl orders, pushing me toward the boat.

"Why did you send me over here just to take me back?" I ask. "And what about my canoe?"

"Never mind the canoe," Carl says, ignoring my first question.

With Carl supporting me, I clamber into the small boat and sit down. Carl unties the mooring rope from the tree, tosses it into the boat and climbs in. I have to hold on to the sides as the boat lurches and the bottom scrapes against the rocks. Carl takes an aluminum paddle from beside his feet and uses it to push the boat away from shore. When we're clear of the rocks, he starts the outboard motor, and we move off.

We cross the water to the mainland much faster than I did in the canoe. Carl runs it aground on the narrow beach by our cabin and helps me out. I guess I'm supposed to be feeling scared at this point in the game, but I'm quite calm. Although I have no idea what's going to happen next, I'm confident that I have worked out at least part of Grandfather's plan. It would be scary to be abducted by a stranger, but I know who Carl is, and he's not very threatening, helping me in and out of the boat.

As we head up to the cabin, I wonder if Grandfather's going to be there, but it's just as silent and deserted as when I left.

"Sit down," Carl says, pointing to the loveseat by the fireplace.

I do as I'm told and ask, "What now?"

"We wait," Carl answers. He's standing in front of me, but his eyes are scanning the cabin, taking in every detail.

"Are you looking for something?" I ask.

"Just be quiet," Carl orders without looking at me. Conversation's obviously not a part of the role he's playing.

I let my gaze wander around the room. It's just as compulsively neat and tidy as Grandfather left it. The only difference I notice is that he has inserted the book he brought from his cottage among the others on the mantel. Oddly, it's not placed in alphabetical order. George Orwell should be in about the middle. Instead, it's third from the left, between Dan Brown and Stephen King. I begin to stand to correct the error, but then the thought pops into my mind that I'm becoming as obsessively tidy as Grandfather is, and I sit back down.

Boredom is beginning to creep over me when I hear footsteps on the porch. I think it might be Grandfather, but when the door opens, Sophie and Carl from Grandfather's cottage are standing there.

I suppose it makes sense that Grandfather would involve both Carl and Sophie in his plan, but I've seen her already, so doesn't her appearance give it all away?

"Hello, Steve," Sophie says with a smile as she steps toward me. "Good to see you again."

"What are you doing here?"

"I've come to find something, and I'm hoping you can help me."

"Tom Thomson's skull?" I ask.

A frown flashes across Sophie's face, but the smile's quickly back in place. "I'm looking for something your grandfather brought up here. I've searched the cottage at Port Carling and it's not there, so he must have brought it with him."

"Why don't you ask him?"

"He won't say, and I don't want to get... unpleasant...just yet."

I can't help but let out a small laugh. If someone in Grandfather's plot is going to get *unpleasant*, Carl seems like a much more convincing candidate than Sophie.

Sophie's reaction shocks me. Without any warning, she violently sweeps the collection of books off the mantel. They crash onto the loveseat beside me in a disordered pile, making me jump. "What did you do that for?" I shout. "They were in order." I know the last statement's dumb, but it's what pops into my surprised brain.

Sophie takes a step forward and leans over me. If it was Carl doing this, it would be threatening, but Sophie's not much taller than me and probably weighs less. "Either your grandfather brought up a lot of money or something small and very valuable, and I need to find it. You can help us or not. It's up to you, but I would strongly recommend helping."

"I can't help," I say. "We didn't bring a suitcase of money up with us."

"What about something small and valuable. Any ideas?"

Immediately an image of the envelope Grandfather quickly stuffed into his pocket when I surprised him at the cottage springs into my mind. I open my mouth to say something, but what should I say? This has all become too complicated. What has happened to a simple trail of clues?

Sophie notices my confused hesitation. "You know something, don't you?"

"I don't know anything," I say, thinking denial is the safest course.

"Search the place," Sophie orders Carl.

With a nod, the big man starts going around the room, systematically opening cupboards and pulling the contents onto the floor and sweeping things off countertops.

"Hey!" I shout, getting to my feet. "What are you doing? Stop it. This is crazy. Grandfather doesn't want you to do this."

I take a step forward, convinced that I can push past Sophie. My confidence evaporates as I find myself staring at a small pistol in Sophie's hand. It must be a fake, but it's a very good one.

I hesitate, and Sophie pushes me back onto the loveseat. She's stronger than she looks. "Don't be stupid," she says.

My shock at the sight of the gun is fading and my anger is returning. "I'm not the one being stupid. You're the ones wrecking this place. This has gone too far. You're wrecking Grandfather's game. You can't scare me with a fake gun."

I make a move to stand up again, but I freeze at the sound of the explosion close to my head. Sophie has her right arm raised, and the gun in her hand is pointing at the roof beams. A thin stream of gray smoke is swirling out of the barrel. "I warned you," Sophie says.

TEN

"What…what's going on?" My heart is racing, my hands are sweaty, and I'm stumbling over my words. "Grandfather would never allow guns."

"I really don't care what your grandfather would or would not allow," Sophie says. She seems satisfied that the gunshot has had the desired effect on me and has tucked the pistol into the belt of her pants. "All I want is what your grandfather brought up here, so tell me where it is or we'll rip this place apart to find it."

"Maybe he has it with him," I suggest. I'm gradually calming down, and my mind is beginning to work once more. "If it's something small you're looking for, he could be keeping it with him, in a pocket."

Sophie shakes her head. "It has to be in here somewhere."

"How can you be certain?"

"Because I've searched him and he doesn't have anything in his pockets."

Now I'm really confused. How could Sophie have searched Grandfather's pockets? Either she's lying and this is all still part of the complex fantasy game created by Grandfather, or...or what? She's really as sinister as she's playing it, and she's kidnapped Grandfather and is holding him hostage somewhere? Or he's lying beaten up—or worse—in the woods somewhere?

Oddly, my confusion helps calm me down. I'm suddenly thinking very clearly, as if my brain knows it needs to focus to work out what is going on and can't afford to let emotions get in the way. Unfortunately, my brain doesn't get much chance to work.

"Hurry up, Jason," Sophie shouts. "Have you found it yet?"

Jason? Carl? Which is his real name? I twist around and see Jason/Carl coming out of Grandfather's bedroom. Looking past him, I see that Grandfather's suitcase is overturned in the corner and his clothes are scattered all over the floor. The room looks as messy as my room at home. The only place left to search is my room, and I know he won't find anything in there. What'll happen then? I need to think, but too much is happening. I need to get away.

"There's nothing in the kid's room," Jason/Carl says.

"I have an idea where Grandfather might have hidden something," I blurt out. I actually don't have any idea—I'm simply making stuff up as I go along. "Back at the cottage, he had an envelope that he didn't want me to see. Maybe that's what you're looking for."

Sophie looks interested in what I'm saying, so I go on. "When we got here, he spent a long time at the woodpile outside. Maybe he hid something there."

I'm hoping this will draw them outside and give me a chance to escape.

"That's a good idea," Sophie agrees. "Jason, go outside and check the woodpile."

This isn't what I'd hoped for. "It's a big wood-pile," I say hurriedly. "It'll take a long time to search it all for an envelope. I could show you where Grandfather was working."

Sophie stares hard at me, and I force myself to keep meeting her eyes, hoping I look inno-cent and eager to be helpful. "Okay," she says. "Show us."

I jump up, wanting to get to the door first, but Sophie grabs my shoulder. "I don't want any nonsense," she says. "You're just a dumb kid. You don't understand what's going on. Just do as you're told."

Now I'm angry. Just a dumb kid who doesn't understand anything! I've been solving mysteries in my head forever. This is Steve McLean the

Super Sleuth she's dealing with. I grunt a reply, shrug her hand off my shoulder and continue to the door.

The door opens outward onto the porch. I open it, walk out, then turn and stand as if I'm a polite kid holding the door open for my elders and betters. Jason/Carl is leading the way. He's saying something over his shoulder to Sophie. As he gets to the door, I throw all my weight against it. It slams shut with a crash. I hear a cry of pain from the other side, but I'm already off the porch and sprinting for the trees.

As I run, I feel an itch in the middle of my back where I know Sophie's bullet will hit. I vaguely wonder if you hear the bullet that kills you, and then I'm in the trees. I keep going, weaving around the trunks and tearing through the underbrush. At last, bent over and gasping for breath, I stop, hoping I've come far enough. I stand still until my breathing slows and my heart stops hammering around inside my chest. I hear nothing. No sounds of pursuit.

I wait until I'm certain no one has followed me and my heartbeat is normal again, and then I work my way slowly back toward the cabin. I feel like one of the trappers or explorers I used to pretend to be in the woods around Grandfather's cottage. I am hyper-aware of everything. Every tree trunk, branch and leaf is sharp and vivid, like a hi-def, 3-D movie, and I'm certain I could hear a butterfly cough six meters away.

Eventually, I reach the edge of the clearing, crouch down and peer at the cabin. I almost give everything away by bursting out laughing. Jason/Carl is awkwardly pulling the woodpile apart with one hand while the other holds a blood-stained rag to his nose. Part of me feels a bit bad. What if this is a game after all, and I've broken an actor's nose? Then Jason/Carl helps me overcome my guilt.

"There's nothing here," he says, grunting in pain. "When I catch that little brat, I'll teach him a lesson."

"Maybe, Jason, if you had paid more attention to the little brat, he wouldn't have had the chance to slam the door in your face," Sophie says without a trace of sympathy in her voice. "And sending him over to the island at this stage was dumb. We had to check this place out first."

"I brought him back," Jason/Carl says defensively.

"And then you let him run away. This is a waste of time. Let's go back and see if McLean will tell us."

"We'll need to put some pressure on him" is the last thing I hear Sophie say as the pair moves around the cabin and down to the shore. They clamber into the red boat and head off along the shore until I lose sight of them behind the trees. For the first time in a while I relax, but so many questions are whirling around my head. Is this a game? If so, it's incredibly elaborate and doesn't seem to be going according to plan. If it's not a game, what is it? Who are Sophie and Jason/Carl?

Where's Grandfather? The final question is worrying. Why isn't he a part of this story, and what did Sophie mean by *put some pressure on him*? Is Grandfather in danger?

ELEVEN

I sit in the shadows of the trees for a long time, staring at the empty cabin. A wind is getting up, and the open front door of the cabin swings mournfully back and forth. It's like my mind swinging between happily working out Grandfather's clues and being totally confused by events that seem to make no sense.

I close my eyes to force back the tears I feel coming. Partly they are tears of frustration, but, if I'm honest with myself, they're also tears of fear. I'm scared. The possibility that Sophie and Jason/ Carl are not part of Grandfather's plan and that

Sophie would actually use the gun she fired in the cabin is terrifying.

The whole thing's made more scary by not knowing why anything is happening and not seeing any way that I can find an answer. It's like someone in a spy story being tortured for vital information. How does the torturer know whether the person being tortured is just strong and refusing to give the information up or genuinely does not know? How does the person being tortured convince the person torturing them that they don't know the information?

James Bond would know what to do. He would find out what's going on, defeat the bad guys, rescue Grandfather and have a happy ending. But I'm not James Bond. I'm just a confused, scared, lonely kid. I would give everything to see Grandfather stroll around the corner of the cabin, walk over to me and explain what is happening.

I open my eyes and wipe the tears away. The clearing's still empty. The door's still swinging in the wind. Grandfather's not going to come and help me. Neither is James Bond. If I'm not going to sit here feeling sorry for myself, I have to do something—but what?

Like all good detectives, before I do anything else I have to think. I sit with my back against a tree trunk, take a deep breath to calm myself and go over what I know.

Grandfather brought me up here and told me the story of Tom Thomson.

He told me he had a mystery for me to solve and that he had prepared clues for me to follow to find Tom Thomson's lost skull.

I discovered and followed the first clue and met Jason/Carl, who gave me the second clue that led me to the island.

Jason/Carl brought me back to the cabin, where Sophie met us.

Sophie was at Grandfather's cottage, apparently discussing arrangements with Grandfather.

Sophie is looking for something valuable, probably the envelope I saw Grandfather put in his pocket at the cottage.

Sophie has a gun!

Sophie implied that they are holding Grandfather somewhere and that they are going to force him to tell them where the valuable package is.

Set out in a list in my head, I know these eight things. They don't all fit together, and some don't seem to make much sense, but they might be parts of two stories. The first three things seem to form one story—the next five seem to form another, although the fifth thing could be a part of the first story. So there are two possibilities.

Possibility one. It's all the same story, and I don't know it. Grandfather has created a much more complicated mystery for me to solve and hasn't told me much about it because he wants me to work it all out myself. This is the sort of thing he would do. He's always saying you can't rely on other people, so the only person you can trust totally in any situation is yourself.

Possibility two. The stories are different, and around the third or fourth thing that happened,

I slipped from one story into the other. This is the scenario that scares me—the possibility that there are sinister people running around with guns who have kidnapped and possibly tortured Grandfather and I have no idea why.

I really want to dismiss possibility two. If it's true, there are just too many questions. Who are these people? Why are they trying to steal something valuable from Grandfather? What sort of things led Grandfather to get involved with these people?

But there are some things that just don't fit with possibility one. Why did Grandfather say I was going to get clues to lead me to an answer when all the clues seem to have stopped? What do Sophie and Jason/Carl have to do with Tom Thomson's skull? Would Grandfather allow Sophie to have a real gun as part of the story?

Okay, I've listed everything I know and I'm still as confused as ever. Maybe I should go and find some help. If there is some ominous plot that hasn't been arranged by Grandfather, the police or at least the park rangers should be told. But what would I tell them? I have no evidence except a messy cabin. Even if they were to find the bullet Sophie fired into the roof beams in the cabin, it proves nothing. As soon as I mention that Grandfather brought me up here to give me a mystery to solve, I'll be dismissed as an overly imaginative kid.

My only other choice is to do something on my own. The idea's frightening, but maybe if I take it slowly I'll be able to collect enough information to convince someone else that something disturbing is going on. Of course, if it's possibility one, I have nothing to worry about whatever I do.

Okay, I'm going to do something, but what? The only clue I can follow is that Sophie and Jason/Carl left in the red boat belonging to the resort. Thinking back, the sound of the outboard motor didn't last long, so I'd put money on them simply using the boat to get back to the resort, which means that they are not that far away.

I like the idea. In a resort there'll be other people around—it'll be safe.

I stand up and step out of the trees. Nothing happens. I edge slowly across the clearing, looking all around. Out on the lake, the wind is picking up and small waves are forming. There's a canoe tossing around about halfway to the island. I peer hard. The canoe's empty. It's my canoe, the one I took over to the island. It must have come loose, and the wind is pushing it back toward the shore. I watch the way it's drifting. The canoe's getting closer, but it's also moving along the shore. I guess it will end up grounding somewhere behind me.

I toy with the idea of following it along the shore and bringing it back, but I know that's just delaying what I have to do. I watch it for a moment or two longer and then continue across the clearing toward the resort.

TWELVE

The gate in the fence around the resort is as firmly locked as it was when I wandered through the trees earlier. I could go around to the main gate on the road, but then what? I could ring the bell and say, *I think there are two people here who have kidnapped my grandfather and are torturing him.* I can't see that getting me inside.

I walk to the shore, hoping the fence doesn't extend right into the water. It does, but it's lower here and fairly beat-up from winter storms on the lake. At one place a large log has come to rest against the fence, bending it over. It's fairly easy to scramble up the log, over the fence and down onto the rocks on the other side. The wind's gotten higher, and the waves are splashing the rocks, making them slippery, but I get onto the resort lawn with only wet feet.

I feel horribly exposed on this side of the fence. There are only a few scattered trees between me and the main resort building. I work my way along the fence and then across the lawn, darting from tree to tree.

The resort is less impressive close up than it is from the road. On the side of the building, there are few windows and only a couple of small doors, which lead, I presume, to the kitchen or service areas. Since a grubby kid in shorts and a T-shirt wouldn't last five seconds walking through the front door of a place like this, the service doors look like my best bet. One door doesn't have a handle on the outside, so I head for the one beside a fenced area containing large garbage and recycling bins. I grab the handle and pull—nothing. I try to turn the handle—still nothing. Then I see the security guard coming around the corner.

I flatten myself against the wall. Fortunately, the guard isn't looking my way. He's scanning the trees I've just passed through. I wonder if I showed up on a security camera and he's been sent out to check. Whether that's the case or not, pretty soon he's going to look along the side of the building, and that'll be it for me.

My only chance is to dash past the garbage bins and around to the back of the building and hope I can get in that way. The trouble is, the guard will almost certainly see me. Maybe I should just walk out into the open and give myself up. The worst that can happen is I get thrown out for trespassing. After all, I don't even have a clear idea of what I am looking for inside.

Then the door beside me opens. Someone carrying a pile of large crushed cardboard boxes staggers out. I freeze, but the person is busy trying to kick a rock over to wedge the door open while not dropping the load of cardboard. I doubt he would see me if I began dancing. Eventually the rock is kicked into place to hold the door open a few inches, and the bundle of cardboard moves off to the recycling bin. I glance at the security guard. He's turning my way. I slide my fingers into the gap, haul the door open and push through. Even if the security guy sees me, I'm hoping he'll think I'm helping take the garbage out.

It takes a moment for my eyes to adjust to the gloom. I'm in a long corridor with bare concrete walls and pipes and cables running along the ceiling. I can't stay here and wait for cardboard guy to return or the security guard to come and investigate, so I head off down the corridor.

There's light at the far end, and I can hear voices and the noise of pots banging. I assume it's the kitchen. I try a door on my right, but it's a storeroom. The next door's an empty office. The third is a walk-in cooler. I reach the fourth door just as the outside door is pulled open. I push against the fourth door and find myself at the bottom of a stairwell.

I sigh with relief and lean against the wall as footsteps pass outside the door. I have to go up the stairs, but my legs feel too weak to do anything. So much for the movies where the cool hero wanders casually through the enemy head-quarters surrounded by heavily armed soldiers intent on killing him. I've come close to getting caught trespassing in a fancy resort by the guy who takes out the garbage, and my heart feels as if it's about to explode out of my chest.

I close my eyes and breathe deeply until I calm down. This is insane. This can't possibly be a part of Grandfather's game—can it? All I can do is continue and see what happens. I creep up the stairs and slowly open the door on the first landing I come to.

I'm in another corridor. This one's much fancier than the one I just left. It has plush carpeting, nice paint on the walls and no pipes running along the ceiling. Doors with fancy scrolled numbers line both sides. I presume these are guest rooms. Short of barging into one at random and destroying the holiday someone has probably paid a lot of money for, there's not much I can do except keep going.

I'm calm now, but that only makes me feel more stupid with every step. What do I think I'm going to find out? What seemed like a good idea when I was sitting against a tree having just escaped from a woman with a gun now seems dumb. My plan was to get in here—and then what? All I'm doing is walking aimlessly along a corridor, leaving wet, muddy footprints on the deep pile carpet. I should just give myself up, get thrown out and head back to the cabin. Grandfather's probably sitting at the table, ready to give me a hard time about being a lousy detective.

I notice a door with no number on it. I'm wondering what it leads to when the next door along, number 135, opens and I hear voices. I grab the handle of the unmarked door. It turns easily, the door opens, and I step through. The old man sitting by the fireplace looks up from the book he's reading. "Have you come to rescue me?" he asks.

THIRTEEN

"What?" I ask.

"Have you come to rescue me?" the old man repeats. He speaks good English but with a heavy accent that I guess is eastern European.

"I don't know," I mumble. Barging into someone's room is bad enough, but then being asked weird questions is unsettling. The idea crosses my mind that the resort sign at the front is old and the place is now being used as an asylum for crazy wealthy people. I turn to leave, but the noise of several people talking in the corridor makes me hesitate.

I look back at the old man. He's grinning. "I think you'd better stay," he says. I push the door closed and inch my way over to the fireplace.

"Sit down. Sit down," the old man says, indicating the other chair by the fire.

I perch on the edge and ask, "What did you mean when you asked if I had come to rescue you? Do you need to be rescued?"

The old man's grin broadens, revealing teeth that are too perfect and white to be real. "We all need rescuing in one way or another. But you are right—I was probably a bit dramatic in the way I phrased my question. I'm waiting for someone to bring me some money so that I can leave this place. I don't suppose that would be you?"

"I'm afraid not," I reply. "Why do you need money to leave this place? It seems to me that you would need money to stay here."

The old man laughs. "A very good point, my young friend, but not all things are always as they seem. And I am being rude." With considerable effort, he hauls himself out of his chair and holds out his hand. "My name is Yuri, Yuri Koval." He looks at me as if the name should mean something.

I stand up and shake his hand. His skin is wrinkled and dry, but his grip is firm. "Pleased to meet you, Mr. Koval," I say. "My name's Steven McLean, but everyone calls me Steve."

"Then you must call me Yuri," the old man says. He tilts his head to one side and stares at me thoughtfully. "Steven McLean," he says as he releases my hand and sits back down. "A good Scottish name, if I am not mistaken. Is that where you are from? Perhaps on a holiday here?"

"My family came over from Scotland several generations ago," I explain, thinking back to a family tree I had to draw in grade five. "I'm here on holiday for a few days with my grandfather."

"Ah," Koval says. "Your grandfather must be quite an old man."

"He's old," I say, "but he keeps himself in good shape."

"I'm sure he does," Koval says. "And you and he are having a good holiday?"

"We've just been here a couple of days," I explain, not certain yet whether my holiday is good or bad.

Koval nods. "But you are not staying in this expensive resort? You are not the type one sees around here."

"We're staying in a cabin on the next lot over." I feel a bit like I'm being interrogated, so I decide to ask a question of my own. "Are *you* here on holiday?"

Koval laughs out loud, a harsh croaking sound that degenerates into a rough cough. When he recovers, he says, "In a sense, yes, I am here on holiday, but it is a holiday I began many years ago."

His next question takes me completely by surprise. "Is your grandfather's name David McLean?"

"Yes," I say. "How did you know that?"

Koval fixes me with an unblinking stare, a half smile turning up the corners of his lips. The stare drags out so long that I'm feeling quite uncomfortable when Koval finally breaks the silence.

"If we ask the right questions and pay attention to the answers, we can learn many things. But now I am thirsty. If you would be so kind, young Steve McLean, would you go through to the kitchen? It is small, but it has a refrigerator below the window within which you will find some of your Canadian beer, for which I have developed a fondness. If you bring me one and a glass from the shelf above, you may help yourself to a soft drink—I think you will find a good selection— and I shall tell you a story that I suspect you will find interesting."

I head through to the tiny kitchen. The window has a view across the lawn to the dock and out over the lake to the island I visited earlier. The wind is still creating waves, and I peer to the right, but there's no sign of the canoe. By now it must have grounded on the shore somewhere. I grab a beer and a can of Coke from the fridge and return to the main room.

Koval pours his beer and takes a long drink. I pop the can of Coke and take a sip. All the confusion I felt before is back. How did I end up in this suite with a mysterious old man who seems to know my grandfather? I must admit that I'm impatient for the story Koval has to tell, but he seems content to sit and stare at the bubbles rising in his beer glass. "Are you Russian?" I ask in an attempt to get Koval started. It works.

"I am not Russian," Koval says sharply. "I am from Ukraine. You've heard of that place?" I nod, although I know almost nothing about it. "A thousand years ago, Ukraine was the most powerful nation in Europe, and Kiev was a wonder of the world. But we are on a crossroads; armies marching east or west passed through Ukraine. We have been conquered in turn by Mongols, Poles, Russians and Germans. We have been slaughtered in wars and starved in famines. Even here in Canada, we were put in internment camps because we were not trusted.

"Recently, the Soviet empire, our most recent invader, collapsed and Ukraine became an independent country. For the first time we had control of our destiny, but we are still on a cross-roads, and we have powerful neighbors. Should we look east, or should we look west, and if we choose one direction, what will our neighbors on the other side do? I think difficult times are ahead for my country. I am an old man, but I wish to go home to help as much as I am able to and be buried in the land where I was born. Is that too much to wish for?"

"No," I say, "but why can't you just go?"

"Life appears simple when you are young, Steven. Many years ago, it seemed that way for me as well. I was certain that I could help my country by passing information to other countries I thought could help us."

"You were a spy?" I ask in shock.

"That is a bit dramatic," Koval says with a tired smile. "I had information and I decided who should know it. So, with the help of another young man, I came to your country, thinking that my information would make a difference. I was wrong, but of course I could not go back home.

Your government let me stay for no charge in this delightful place, so I have lived here ever since. My needs are catered to and I am given a small allowance, but I have no savings and so I cannot travel far.

"Now, I do not blame your government for keeping me here—they have been generous enough, and it *was* my decision to come here—but now things are different in my home. It will be safe for me to return, and I wish to do so. Your government does not wish to help me, and so I contacted the man who helped me before, and he agreed to assist me once more by supplying the funds to make my return possible. I think you can guess who that man was and is."

It takes me a moment to work out what Koval means, but then it hits me like a freight train. "Grandfather?"

Koval nods and takes another drink of his beer. "Yes, Steven. The one I hope will assist me in getting home is your grandfather, David McLean."

FOURTEEN

I stare at Koval and try to work out how the story he has told me fits in with my grandfather, who brought me here on a road trip and set up a mystery for me to solve around Tom Thomson's missing skull. That much I am sure of. What I'm not sure of is everything else.

Is Grandfather really involved with Koval and using our trip as a cover to bring him money so he can get home? Are Sophie and Jason/Carl really trying to steal that money? Have I misunderstood clues in the game Grandfather set up for me and stumbled into this? Or is it all a much more elaborate game than Grandfather told me?

"Do you know anything about Tom Thomson?" I ask, hoping to surprise Koval into a reaction.

It doesn't work. Koval casually drains his beer glass and says, "It is impossible to live around here and not know that name. Every year new people come here with a new conspiracy theory about his death."

"What do you think happened to him?"

Koval shrugs. "I always believe the simplest answer. I think he died in a fishing accident and his body was moved home, where he is buried today. Anything else is unprovable and too complicated. But I have a question for you. If you did not bring the money from your grandfather, why has he not come himself to see me?"

It's a good question, and one I can't answer. So I ask another one. "Do you know a woman called Sophie or a guy called Jason or Carl?"

"The names mean nothing," Koval says with a vague wave of his empty glass. "Fetch me another beer, please, Steven, while I think on what this all might mean."

I do as Koval asks. As I straighten up, I glance out the window and almost drop the bottle. Three figures are on the dock, getting ready to go out in the red boat—Sophie, Jason/Carl and my grandfather. I stare for a moment as Sophie starts the outboard motor and then I turn and dash back through to the main room.

"They're leaving! They've got Grandfather! I have to go!" I yell as I head for the door. On the way, I drop the beer on Koval's chair. I hear him shout after me, "Good luck!"

This time I don't care who sees me going through the resort. I tear along the corridor, narrowly missing a startled waiter pushing a trolley laden with drinks and snacks. The corridor opens into a wide atrium, and I skid to a halt on the polished tile floor to get my bearings. To my left is a long reception desk where an old couple is signing in while a bored porter leans on a cart stacked high with pink suitcases.

To my right several people are sitting in plush chairs, sipping expensive-looking drinks. Several turn their heads to look at me. On the other side of the drinkers is a set of glass doors leading onto an outside patio, the lawn, the dock and a view of the red boat bumping its way over the waves toward the island.

I head for the doors. A waiter steps forward and politely asks if he can help me. "No, thanks," I say as I sidestep him, cross the patio in half a dozen strides and hurtle down the lawn. By the time I'm on the dock, the red boat is almost at the island.

"Stop!" I yell as loudly as I can, but it's hopeless. There's no way they can hear me at that distance and over the roar of the outboard. I wave frantically, but no one notices except the waiter, who has followed me down from the patio. "I think you should leave now, sir," he says.

"Right," I say as I push past him, an idea forming in my mind. I sprint along the shore and scramble over the fence. I glance over at the island, where Jason/Carl is tying up the boat as the others climb out onto the shore. Then I keep running.

By the time I get to the beached canoe, I'm struggling for breath and battered and scratched from running through the underbrush. The canoe has come to a stop wedged between a pair of rocks. There's a couple of inches of water in the bottom, but I'm relieved to see that the paddle and life vest are still there. I put on the life vest and stand on a rock, knee deep in cold lake water, while I haul the canoe off the rocks. Getting in without tipping is tricky, but I manage and begin paddling toward the island.

The going is hard against the wind and the waves, and the water in the bottom of the canoe makes it tippy. I look around for a bailer, but there's nothing, so I have no choice but to keep going.

What was a pleasant paddle earlier in the day seems to take forever, and my arms are aching and I'm soaked by the spray by the time I get close to the island. I turn the canoe so the prow faces straight at the shore, but that's a mistake. It means that the canoe is now side-on to the waves. A particularly large one catches me full-on. The canoe tips, the water sloshes over to one side, I lose my balance, and suddenly I'm swallowing lake water.

My head breaks the surface, and I cough and splutter. The canoe is beside me, upside down, and there's no way I can turn it over on my own. I feel panic rising. Am I to end up like Tom Thomson, a drowned corpse found floating in the lake days later? I try screaming for help but only succeed in swallowing another mouthful of water. I kick my legs wildly—and stub my toe on a rock.

The pain seems to calm my fright. I feel around with my feet until I find a rock to stand on. The shore is quite close; so is the canoe. I launch myself off the rock and grab the overturned hull. With a combination of kicking and pushing off underwater rocks, I edge toward the shore. Soon I can place both feet on the bottom. It's a struggle, and I stumble a lot on the slippery rocks, but I manage to drag the canoe to shore and partly out of the water. I don't have the strength or interest to turn it over or try and find a place to tie it up. I clamber over the rocks and lean against a tree to catch my breath and decide what to do next.

I'm sheltered from the wind, but I'm soaked through, and heavy clouds are building, blocking any sunlight. I begin to shiver. From somewhere in the recesses of my tired brain, I drag up a fun fact that Sam once told me—most people don't get hypothermia in the winter, when they tend to wear lots of clothing. The danger of chilling your body enough to be in danger is greatest in August, when people are taken by surprise by an accident and are dressed for warm weather, such as a T-shirt and shorts. It's August, I've just been surprised by an accident, and I'm wearing only a T-shirt and shorts.

"Thanks, Sam," I murmur as I jump up and down and flail my arms to try to warm up.

FIFTEEN

Waving my arms helps a bit, but I still can't stop shivering. I need to get moving. I know Grandfather's on the island and possibly in danger, but where? Looking around, I notice that I am close to the spot where Jason/Carl tied up the red boat when he came to take me back to the mainland. After a few moments' searching, I find the path leading into the trees.

It feels good to be doing something, but I wish I had more of a plan. The island's quite large and heavily treed. There's a lot of land to search and plenty of places to hide if someone doesn't want to be found. All I can do is try.

There are no roads on the island, but it's crisscrossed with paths, some of which are little more than deer trails that I have to push my way through. Pretty soon I have lost all sense of direction and am simply walking trails at random. Occasionally I stumble into a clearing, sometimes the same clearing several times. All the while, I'm getting colder and more discouraged. Eventually I huddle down against a tree beside the trail and hug my legs to my chest to try and conserve heat. I'll just rest for a minute or two before going on. I feel totally miserable and wish that Grandfather had never come up with the dumb idea of taking his grandsons on special trips. I'd give anything to be warm and back home. I'd even happily spend the week playing Warhammer with Sam and his nerdy friends. Just when things can't get any worse, thunder rumbles in the distance, and it begins to rain.

The large raindrops from the approaching storm make quite the noise, splashing through the trees. That's probably why I don't hear the man coming up behind me until I feel his hand on my shoulder.

Despite my misery and exhaustion, I leap to my feet and spin around. The man is tall and strongly built. His head is shaved, and he has a dark beard. Fortunately, he's smiling.

"You look kind of cold," he says, stating the obvious in a broad American accent. "D'you know more people get hypothermia in August than in January?"

"I know," I stammer through chattering teeth, wondering if I've been discovered by one of Sam's relatives.

The man takes off his jacket, wraps it around my shoulders and pulls the hood up. It's about five sizes too big for me, but it has a fleece lining and it's still warm from his body heat. I pull it tight around me and instantly feel better.

"Thanks," I say.

"No problem. What're you doing wandering around these woods with a storm coming on?"

"My canoe tipped in the wind," I say.

The man nods. "Shipwreck," he says. "People tend to take the lake for granted, but it can be treacherous, especially at this time of year when thunderstorms come through. They seem to appear from nowhere sometimes." As if to emphasize what he's saying, thunder crashes deafeningly overhead. "You look a bit better," the man says. "You feel warmer?"

I nod weakly.

"Would some hot chocolate improve the situation even more?"

I nod harder.

"Let's go then. I've got a cabin at the south end of the island. There are dry clothes there as well. I suspect they'll be a bit large for you, but better than nothing."

My savior strides off down the trail and I follow. I've almost stopped shivering, but my feet feel like lumps of ice. My companion doesn't seem to mind that he has given up his jacket. He's striding along so fast that I almost have to run to keep up. "My name's Steve," I say in an effort to engage him in conversation and slow him down. "What's yours?"

"Carl," he says over his shoulder without breaking stride.

I stop dead in my tracks and stare at the man's back as he keeps going along the trail. He *could* be the figure I glimpsed at Grandfather's cabin. But if this is Carl, who's the guy with Sophie? "Wait," I shout as I begin to run. "Did you say Carl?"

"Common name," the guy says.

I've almost caught up to him when we burst out into a small clearing. Through the driving rain, I can see a cabin, much nicer than the one Grandfather and I are in. Behind it is a dock where two boats bob, one of which is the red one from the resort. I don't have the time or energy to work out what this means because Carl strides up to the cabin and pushes the door open. I stumble in behind him. The first thing I see around Carl's imposing bulk is a wonderful fire crackling in the hearth. Then I see that we're not alone.

Three figures are standing in the middle of the room. "It took you long enough to get here," Grandfather says with a smile.

I want to run to him, but Carl places a firm hand on my shoulder. Grandfather, giving me a broad wink, steps over to stand beside Carl.

Sophie is standing a couple of paces in front of me with Jason, as I think of her companion now, behind her. His nose is red and looks like it hurts. Neither one seems happy to see us. "What are you doing here?" Sophie asks.

I can't answer because I have no clue what's going on, but Grandfather says, "It didn't work out the way you wanted, Sophie, but the game's over now."

"Not yet," Sophie replies, her face twisted in anger. She raises her hand, and I see she's holding the pistol she fired in the cabin. "The game's not over until I say it's over. Tell me where the money's hidden."

"The pistol won't do you any good now." Grandfather shakes his head. "It really is over. And I have to get my grandson some dry clothes and something hot to drink so he can warm up."

Sophie raises her arm higher and points the gun at Grandfather. "I'm finished with your games," she says. "I'm deadly serious. I want that money." For a moment we stand like a group of figures in a wax museum, Sophie front and center and angry, Jason in the background, looking worried, Carl standing calmly beside me, Grandfather relaxed and smiling, and me just wanting to get out of my wet clothes and hunker down in front of the roaring fire.

Someone has to do something. "Sophie," I say, shrugging off Carl's hand and taking a step forward. Sophie half turns toward me. The gun moves away from Grandfather. I don't think. I just leap. Well, *leap*'s not the right word. It's more a couple of stumbling steps before I trip on the hem of Carl's vast jacket. I cannon into Sophie's legs. She yells in surprise and falls heavily backward across the coffee table in front of the fire. Her arms flail wildly and the pistol flies in a wide arc to land at Jason's feet. He stares at it uncertainly for a moment, picks it up and waves it about as if trying to decide who to point it at.

"Be careful, Jason," Sophie says from the floor beside me. "It has a hair trigger."

Jason glances down at Sophie. "We can still get the money," he says. He points the gun at Grandfather and pulls the trigger.

SIXTEEN

The explosion of the gunshot is just as loud as the one in the other cabin earlier in the day and leaves my ears ringing. The difference is that this time Grandfather's been shot. I scream in horror and jump to my feet. Grandfather's still standing beside Carl, smiling at me. Why isn't he on the floor in a spreading pool of blood?

Jason is staring stupidly at the gun in his hand. "I didn't mean to shoot," he says. Carl steps forward and takes the gun from Jason's unresisting grip.

Sophie struggles to her feet. "What happened?" she asks.

"Blanks," Grandfather says. "You don't think I'd let you run around near my grandson with a loaded gun, do you?"

"But how did you…?"

"Enough for now," Grandfather says. "I told you the game was over." He turns to Carl. "The worst of the weather's probably past now. These summer thunderstorms never last long. Perhaps you could take Sophie and Jason back over to the mainland while I find some dry clothes for Steven. I imagine he has some questions."

"Sure thing," Carl says. "Can I have my jacket back?"

In a daze I hand Carl his jacket and watch as he hustles the other two out of the cabin. Boy, do I have questions.

"Get over by the fire," Grandfather tells me, "and take off those wet clothes. I'll find some dry ones and see if I can fix us a hot drink."

"Carl said there was hot chocolate," I suggest.

"Perfect," Grandfather says.

* * *

It's amazing how feeling comfortable can change your view of the world. A short time ago I was cold, scared and confused. I'm still confused, but I feel safe and warm. I'm dressed in clothes that are ridiculously big for me, but they're dry, and the heat from the fire is warming my bones. Best of all, I'm clasping a large steaming mug of hot chocolate. It even has marshmallow bits floating in it.

"So, you have some questions," Grandfather says as he sits down across from me.

"No kidding," I say. "I spent half of today convinced I had everything worked out and the other half terrified that I was caught in some vast, dangerous plot I don't understand. What's going on?"

Grandfather laughs. "I imagine it has been a bit confusing for you, but before I answer your questions, can you tell me in detail what happened to you today?"

"Sure." Between sips of hot chocolate, I go over the day. I tell him about working out the first clue, meeting Jason, going over to the island, being brought back to the cabin, where Sophie fired the gun in the air, going to the resort to try to rescue Grandfather, stumbling into Koval's room, seeing Grandfather being taken to the island, and my adventure with the canoe. It's comforting to say it all out loud, but it doesn't make any more sense than it did before.

Grandfather nods encouragement occasionally as I talk. When I finish, he stares intently into the fire, concentrating hard. I sit patiently, happy to luxuriate in the warmth and comfort. I catch myself nodding off just before Grandfather looks up at me and begins his explanation.

"The first, and most important, thing you need to know is that I messed up. Yes, I set up this mystery game for you, and I didn't tell you all the details before it began, but I feel terrible that you were put in danger, and I apologize from the depths of my heart for that."

"It's okay," I say. "Everything's turned out fine."

"It's kind of you to forgive me, but I must take responsibility for what happened. The other thing I want to say right up front is that I am immensely proud of you and how you handled yourself in very difficult circumstances. You didn't panic, and you kept thinking. You kept looking for solutions, and that's an admirable quality that will serve you well throughout your life."

"Thank you," I say softly. Grandfather doesn't have to know about the terror I felt when Sophie fired the pistol or when the canoe overturned.

"Having said that," Grandfather goes on, "what you did in this cabin was incredibly dumb. Distracting Sophie and throwing yourself at her when she had the pistol pointing at me was astonishingly brave, but dumb."

"The gun was loaded with blanks," I say defensively. "You said that."

"I did say that," Grandfather agreed, "but only after it had all happened. You didn't know there were only blanks in the gun when you acted. That's what makes your actions brave—and dumb. And you went about it the wrong way. When someone's waving a gun about and you decide you have no choice but to take them on, go for the gun, not the person. There's no point in knocking the person over if they then shoot you. Grab the gun and hold on to it as if your life depends on it, because it probably does."

I nod. That makes sense. Then I ask, "How do you know that? Have you ever had to do that?"

"No, of course not," Grandfather says. "I read it in a book somewhere. Now, to get on with explaining your day. Several things went wrong, and the first one was because of you."

"Because of me? What did I do wrong?"

"You did nothing wrong. In fact, it went wrong because you did something too right. As I said I would, I set out several clues for you to follow. I made them more complicated as they went on, but the first one was very simple. Do you remember it?"

"Yes," I say. "It was on the scrap of paper in the Nero Wolfe book. It said *Begin at the beginning. The third along. Check the empty space at the front.*"

"Well remembered, and you worked out that it referred to the third lot along the lakeshore, the empty one." I nod and Grandfather goes on. "Good work, except I wasn't being that clever. You noticed that I arranged the books on the mantel in alphabetical order by author name."

"Yes," I say, a sinking feeling forming in my stomach.

"And the beginning of the alphabet is *A*…"

"And the third book along was the one you brought up from the cottage."

"And the second clue was on a piece of paper tucked inside the front cover."

"So I wasn't supposed to go to the vacant lot at all?"

"Not then. That's why Jason looked so surprised to see you. You got there just as he was arriving to add a later clue where you would find it.

He panicked and told you to go over to the island. You weren't supposed to go there until much later. That was why he had to go over and bring you back."

"So it's my fault it all went wrong?" I say, feeling miserable that I spoiled Grandfather's elaborate game.

"Not at all. In fact, you did brilliantly. It's not at all your fault that you interpreted the first clue the way you did. It's my fault for giving you a clue that could be understood in more than one way. Shall I top up the hot chocolate before we continue?"

"Yes, please," I say, glad of a breathing space to absorb what I've been told already.

SEVENTEEN

As Grandfather pokes around in the kitchen, I think about what he has told me. My misinterpretation of the first clue makes sense, but there's still a lot that doesn't. I try to fit it all together, but I'm tired and my brain isn't working as well as it should, so I'm glad when Grandfather returns with more hot chocolate to tell me the rest of the tale. "Where did the second clue lead me?" I ask when he has settled back down in his chair.

"The second clue told you to go to the resort next door and ask to speak to Mr. Koval."

"He was a part of the game?"

"Of course," Grandfather says. "Everyone was, but because you misinterpreted the first clue, you began to do things in the wrong order. Yuri was supposed to tell you to go to the vacant lot next door, where you would find the next clue. That one would lead you over to the island, where a map in a bottle would lead you this way."

"The Coke bottle I found on the point?"

"Yes, but we never had the chance to put the map in it. On your way down here, Sophie and Jason were supposed to pretend to kidnap you and then allow you to escape here, where you would find the last clue that would tell you where the skull was hidden."

"So none of the stuff about you bringing something valuable up here so that Mr. Koval could get back to the Ukraine and Sophie and Jason wanting to steal it was true?"

Grandfather shakes his head. "Are you sad about that?"

"A little bit," I say. "It was a good story."

"Not bad," Grandfather agrees, "especially since we had to make most of it up on the spur of the moment. Yuri came up with much of it when we discovered what had happened at the vacant lot. As you may have noticed, Yuri loves to tell stories. We decided that I should become the pretend kidnap victim, and your task would be to rescue me. Of course, we didn't allow for the thunderstorm springing up so quickly. Carl came within an ace of jumping in to save you when the canoe tipped, but he saw you were managing and left you to it. When you got lost in the woods and were in danger of becoming hypothermic, he stepped in."

"Who's Carl?"

"He's the son of an American friend who comes up here from time to time to go wilderness trekking. Carl's a survival expert, and he's been your minder all through this adventure. He's shadowed you everywhere, making certain you were never in any real danger."

I think back to unexplained noises I've heard and shadowy forms I've thought I glimpsed out of the corner of my eye. "There were times I wish I had known he was nearby and looking out for me," I say.

"I imagine there were, and I'm sorry for having put you through that. It was never my intention to scare you—well, not too much," he adds with a grin.

"Who are Sophie and Jason?"

"Sophie's the granddaughter of another friend of mine. She's training to be an actress at Ryerson University, so I thought she'd be perfect for the role."

"She was very convincing," I agree.

"Occasionally a bit too convincing," Grandfather says. "As they say in the theater, she inhabited the role. Personally, I thought she took it a bit far, but she felt she had to overdo it in order to convince you after you spotted her by accident at the cottage—she and Carl don't shovel my snow, by the way. I had to make that up on the spur of the moment when you came unexpectedly around the corner of the cottage.

We should have been more careful about my meeting Sophie. Jason's her boyfriend. I didn't particularly want him involved, but Sophie insisted she needed more help, so we brought him in as the heavy."

"You went to a lot of trouble for this," I say.

"I never doubted that you were worth it," Grandfather says. "I'm just sorry it didn't go as smoothly as planned."

"It certainly made it more exciting than the game of Clue I was expecting."

"It did that. Have I explained everything to your satisfaction?"

"I still have a few questions," I say.

"Fire away."

"If Sophie overreacted and Carl was looking after me, why didn't he respond when he heard the gunshot in the cabin?"

"Because he didn't hear it," Grandfather says. "He was in the resort talking with me and Yuri. Jason sending you over to the island and then bringing you back threw us for a loop. At that point we were ad-libbing and busy working out an alternative story for you."

I nod. It makes sense. "Was it coincidence that I stumbled into Yuri's suite at the resort?"

"Partly. Carl was talking to the security guard when he saw you come through the trees on the monitors. When the guard went to check you out, Carl saw you come through the door by the garbage. He knew you were most likely to come up the stairs. It was either that or end up in the kitchen, so he ran upstairs and warned me. We were in room 135. When we heard you come along the corridor, we made a lot of noise, hoping you would try to escape through the only unmarked door, the one to Yuri's room."

"It worked," I say. "Why didn't Yuri's suite have a number?"

"He's a permanent resident at the resort. Those rooms don't have numbers. Any more questions?"

"When we stopped at the cottage, I saw you pick up an envelope. It seemed as if you were trying to hide it, and then Sophie said she was looking for something small and very valuable. What was in the envelope that you didn't want me to see?"

"Well done—you're very observant," Grandfather says as he reaches into his jacket pocket and pulls out a rectangular envelope. "I picked these up the afternoon before we set off. I thought they might make a nice reward for solving the clues I gave you, but you're going to have to earn them. I have one more task for you."

"As long as it doesn't involve guns or falling out of a canoe," I say.

"You should be able to do most of it sitting in your chair. Look in the right pocket of the pants I brought you."

Puzzled, I reach into the pocket and feel a piece of paper. As I pull it out Grandfather asks, "Was that your last question?"

"Almost," I say. "Was the story you told about meeting the fisherman who had Tom Thomson's skull true?"

Grandfather smiles. "Read the piece of paper. It's the last clue."

I unfold the paper and read a short poem written in Grandfather's precise handwriting.

> *Congratulations, Super Sleuth,*
> *You've questioned, sought and learned.*
> *There's one more clue to reach the truth*
> *And win the prize you've earned.*

> *It's tiring work to solve each clue.*
> *Perhaps it's time for bed.*
> *Sleep freshens brains and makes us new*
> *And helps us get ahead.*

I read the poem three times but still can't work out a hidden meaning. "What does it mean?" I ask.

"You must be tired. It's a well-known fact that we need sleep to help our brains refresh themselves. That's why you should always try to get a good sleep before an exam at school. Maybe you need to lie down."

"I am tired," I say, "but this isn't our cabin, and it's beginning to get dark. Shouldn't we be heading back?"

"We'll stay here tonight. Carl says there's food in the fridge and he'll come and pick us up tomorrow. Now go and have a nap while I get supper organized. Your room's the one on the right."

It's odd that Grandfather is ordering me around, but I'm too tired to worry. I haul myself out of the chair and head to the bedroom. I know I shouldn't be surprised, but I scream when I see the grinning skull sitting on the pillow. Then I laugh out loud as I remember the last two lines of the poem. *Sleep freshens brains and makes us new/ And helps us get ahead.* I've just gotten a head!

EIGHTEEN

"Is that really Tom Thomson's skull?" I ask once I've calmed down and returned to the main room.

"I wish I could say yes," Grandfather says, "but it's only a replica from Skulls Unlimited."

"Skulls Unlimited? You're kidding, right?"

"No, they're the go-to place for skulls. You can get real or replica skulls of just about anything, from dinosaurs to humans. I could have got a real human skull, but they're expensive."

"And kind of creepy," I add.

"I guess so," Grandfather agrees. "Bring the skull here and I'll show you something interesting."

I fetch the skull. It's incredibly detailed and looks very old, but it feels light.

"This is a replica of a Roman gladiator's skull," Grandfather explains. "The original is almost two thousand years old and is in a museum in Rome. See this?" He points to a rough area above the right eye socket. "This is a healed wound, probably one suffered in the arena. This man may have fought for his life in the Coliseum in front of Roman emperors, maybe even Hadrian or Marcus Aurelius."

"Cool," I say, turning the skull around in my hands. It's certainly very interesting, but it's not the answer to a mystery I failed to solve.

I guess a look of disappointment must show on my face. "I'm sorry it's not Tom Thomson," Grandfather says. "The story about meeting the fisherman is true, and his cabin did burn down, but I have no idea whether he told me the truth about Thomson's skull or not. I just thought I could elaborate on the story to create the game for you."

"I guess not all mysteries are solvable," I say.

"Life is not like a Nero Wolfe mystery. Often there is no answer—and that's a good thing. Sometimes the most interesting mysteries turn out to have the most boring answers. It's more fun not to know."

Grandfather hands me the envelope. "Here you are. It didn't all work out as I planned, but you've certainly earned this."

I take the envelope, wondering what else Grandfather has in store for me. I pull open the flap and two tickets drop out—tickets to the Foo Fighters next month at the Molson Amphitheatre.

For a moment I'm speechless, so Grandfather fills the silence. "Tickets to that concert you wanted to go to. One for you and one for your friend Sam."

"Wow. Thanks," I say, still feeling overwhelmed. "But Mom said we couldn't go on our own."

"I've cleared it with your mother," Grandfather says with a smile. "Besides, you won't be going on your own." For a moment I have the horrific thought that Grandfather's going to come with us. The only thing worse than not going to see the Foo Fighters would be going with my grandfather. "I'd come myself," Grandfather goes on, "but I don't think I'd fit in. Apparently, Carl is a big fan, and he's offered to go with you boys."

"That's awesome," I say with relief. "Thank you."

"You're welcome," Grandfather says, standing up. "I'm going to see what Carl left us for supper. You must be hungry."

"Starving," I say. "I haven't eaten anything since a bowl of cereal this morning."

"And you've had a busy day. After the meal we should get some sleep. I thought tomorrow we might go and poke around at the old Mowat Cemetery. Maybe see if we can find Tom Thomson's grave."

"Okay," I say, "but if we find it, we're not digging it up."

* * *

The rest of the week at Canoe Lake is fun. Grandfather and I visit Mowat Cemetery but don't find Tom Thomson's grave. We do some canoeing around the islands and a little fishing, and in the evenings Grandfather tells me stories or I read *Fer-de-Lance*. I never see Sophie or Jason again. Grandfather says they have headed back south and that Sophie says she is sorry if she scared me.

I do see quite a lot of Carl. He drops by several times, and on the last three days of the week he takes me on a wilderness canoe trip, which involves taking everything we need with us and portaging between lakes. One afternoon I catch two trout that we have for supper. Around the evening fires, Carl tells me stories about hiking he has done in Yellowstone Park and California and we discuss the Foo Fighters. I'm really looking forward to going to the concert with him.

On the last morning before we leave for home, Grandfather and I are sitting at the table finishing breakfast. "I have a favor to ask you," Grandfather says. "Have you finished reading *Fer-de-Lance*?"

"Yeah," I say. "I enjoyed it. I think I'll try the other Nero Wolfe stories."

"Excellent. Would you mind terribly if we left the book for Yuri? He loves reading, and he's run out of books. He has more on order, but it takes some time for them to be delivered. I'll replace your copy with a newer one if you want to collect the set."

I don't have to think long. I liked the old man in the resort, and I'd rather have a newer copy anyway. "No problem," I say, "but didn't you say it was special to you?"

"I did, but books are meant to be read. Would you mind taking it over to him? I'm sure he'd like to say goodbye. He doesn't get many visitors."

"Sure," I say, quite happy to go and have a wander around the resort without feeling I am about to be chased out.

"You might as well take this one too," Grandfather adds, standing and taking his copy of *Homage to Catalonia* from its place among the others on the mantel. "We'll throw the stuff in the Jeep when you get back and hit the road. If you're not in a hurry, I thought we might take a detour to Leith and visit Thomson's other grave. That way we can be fairly sure we've paid our respects to at least part of the famous artist."

"That'd be good," I say.

I take the books and head for the resort. This time I don't climb the fence but head for the road and enter by the impressive gates. At the reception desk in the foyer, I ask to see Yuri Koval.

The woman behind the desk looks a bit confused and says, "Why do you want to see him?"

It seems an odd question to ask at a resort, but I don't have a good sense of how rich people live, so I say, "I've brought him a couple of books."

"Well, if you give them to me, I'll see that he gets them."

"Thank you," I say, even more confused, "but I'm leaving today, and I'd like to say goodbye."

The woman looks me up and down and obviously isn't impressed by what she sees. "Mr. Koval is in our long-term-stay wing. You'll need to be escorted."

This is getting stranger and stranger, but I shrug and say, "Whatever."

The woman makes a quick phone call, and after a few minutes a security guy shows up. I'm pretty certain it's the one who was chasing me a week ago when I snuck in, and I hope he didn't get a good look at me. All he says is, "This way," and heads off down a corridor.

I follow until we reach a locked door and the security guy has to stop, enter a code into a keypad and lead me through. I think it's odd that there are locked doors in a resort, but what do I know about these places?

Once through the door, we're in the corridor I recognize as the one with Koval's suite.

The security guard knocks, opens the door and ushers me in. "I'll be out here," he says.

Koval is sitting in exactly the same place as before. He has reading glasses balanced on his nose and a large book open on his lap. "Hello, Mr. Koval," I say.

"Yuri," he says, looking up and smiling. "I tell you, call me Yuri. How are you, Steven?"

"I'm fine, thank you. Did your book order arrive sooner than you expected?"

"My book order?"

"Grandfather said you'd run out of books and your order hadn't arrived yet," I say, nodding at the book on his lap.

"Ah, my book order. No, this I borrowed from a friend."

"Well, I've brought you a couple more," I say, handing over *Fer-de-Lance* and *Homage to Catalonia*. "They're a bit old, but I enjoyed *Fer-de-Lance*. It's a mystery."

"Sometimes old is very good," Yuri says, taking the books, "and I enjoy mysteries." He holds the books lovingly, gently stroking the dust jackets. Then he looks up at me. "Please thank your grandfather very much for these. I am eternally in his debt."

This seems a little extreme for a gift of a couple of old books, but then, Yuri's a bit strange. "I hope you enjoy them."

"Oh, I shall," Yuri says, "and thank you for bringing them over. You see, you did come here to rescue me."

"What do you mean?" I ask.

He waves the books. "Now I can escape."

"Escape?"

"Into the world of stories," Yuri says. "I find that a good book can take one to many different places." He stands up and shakes my hand. "Thank you again," he says.

My escort is waiting outside in the corridor and leads me back to the front entrance. As I leave, I turn and say, "Thank you."

"You're welcome," he replies. "Coming in by the front door's much easier, isn't it?"

By the time I've worked out what he said, he's turned away and taken several steps across the lobby. So he did recognize me.

* * *

With only a brief stop in Huntsville to check out the bronze statue of Tom Thomson painting by his overturned canoe, we're in Leith by lunchtime. The large granite slab marking Thomson's grave is easy to find. We stand in front of it and read the inscription.

TOM THOMSON
LANDSCAPE PAINTER
DROWNED IN CANOE LAKE
JULY 8, 1917, AGED 39 YEARS
11 MONTHS 3 DAYS

"Do you think his skull's in there?" I ask.
"More than likely," Grandfather says.
As we walk back to the Jeep, Grandfather

says, "I don't think we should mention too much about this trip to your mother. I don't think she'd be too happy with me if she knew I'd let you fall in the lake in a storm and introduced you to people who waved a gun around, even if it was loaded with blanks."

"I guess not," I say.

"We'll keep it our secret."

"Like the secret of what happened in Central America with DJ?" I say.

"Exactly," Grandfather says with a wink. "Now let's see if there's a place around here that serves a decent pulled-pork sandwich."

NINETEEN

When we get home, Grandfather and Mom sit down for a cup of tea. I excuse myself and go into my room to call Sam. "We're going to the concert," I say as soon as he picks up.

"Where were you?" he asks.

"Didn't you hear what I said?" I ask, surprised by Sam's lack of enthusiasm. "Grandfather got us tickets to the Foo Fighters and someone to take us. We're going to the best concert of the decade!"

"Yeah yeah," Sam says. "I've been trying to call you all week."

"I was on a road trip, Sam. You knew that. There was no cell reception where we were."

"The old book your grandfather gave you, *Fer-de-Lance*—did you read it?"

"Yeah, but what does—?"

"Your grandfather got the book in 1934, right?" Sam interrupts and then goes on without giving me a chance to answer his question. "Did you notice if there was a logo of a flower on the inside?"

"Yes to both questions. So what?"

"The date and the logo mean he gave you a first edition. There's one for sale right now on AbeBooks for $25,000. According to something called *The Book Collector's Magazine*, it could be worth a lot more."

I stare at my phone. Sam's saying that the book Grandfather gave me is worth a fortune. That can't be right. He must have made a mistake. Sam does tend to go off wildly in all directions.

Before I can say anything, Sam says, "We're going to be rich."

"Calm down, Sam," I say. "First off, *we* are not going to be rich. Grandfather gave the book to me, not you. Second, I don't have the book anymore.

"After I read the book," I say to fill the deafening silence on the other end of the phone, "Grandfather asked me to give it and another old book he'd brought to an old guy at the resort beside where we were staying." As I say this, a tiny dark cloud of doubt begins to gather in my mind.

"Another old book?" Sam asks before I can take my doubts any further. "What was it?"

"It was called *Homage to Catalonia*," I say. "By a guy called George…Orwell."

The following silence is broken by the sound of Sam's fingers on his keyboard. I know what he's doing: looking up Orwell's book on the Web. As I wait, I think about what this might mean. If *Fer-de-Lance* and Orwell's book are worth thousands, does that mean there really was something going on behind Grandfather's organized game? If Yuri Koval's story about needing money to get back home were true, and if Grandfather knew that and also that someone else wanted to steal the money, what better way to take the money than as something valuable, and what better things to take than a couple of old books no one would look twice at? If Sophie and Jason were really trying to steal the money, they would be looking for cash or something obvious, like a piece of jewelry or a precious stone.

"When was it published?" Sam breaks into my thoughts.

"No idea," I say. "How much is it worth?"

"Somewhere between $54 and $20,000," Sam says.

"That's not much help, Sam."

"Hey, I do the best I can. If you hadn't given the book away, we could find out."

"I didn't give the book away—Grandfather did. Never mind. I'll go ask him."

"If we are rich, I'm going to buy the best Warhammer tabletop in the world. I've found a post-apocalypse city on eBay. It's got twenty four ruined buildings in six street layouts. It's only $750. It'd be a good start—I'm just saying."

"Sam, like I said before, you were never going to be rich."

"I thought we were friends," Sam says. "What's mine is yours and what's yours is mine."

"But you don't have anything."

"Okay, but if I did, it'd be yours."

"Goodbye, Sam. I'll call you later."

Thanks to Sam, my doubts about whether I was involved in a game or a real mystery have returned. I guess there's only one way to find out. I slide off my bed and head to the kitchen. Both Grandfather and Mom look up and smile. There's nothing to do but launch straight in. "The book you gave me is worth a fortune," I blurt out. "Thousands of dollars."

"Oh, I doubt that." Grandfather shakes his head gently. "It's just an old book."

"Sam looked it up on Wikipedia," I push on. "It's a first edition, and there's one for sale on AbeBooks for $25,000. The other book,

Homage to Catalonia, might be worth $20,000 as well."

"Is this true, Dad?" my mom asks. "Could Sam have made a mistake?" she adds, turning to me.

"Sam didn't make a mistake," I say.

"I'm sure he didn't," Grandfather says, "but the book business is not as simple as perhaps he thinks it is. In fact, it's very complicated. To be worth the sort of money you're talking about, a book has to be in absolutely perfect condition, never read, protected from sunlight and so forth."

"Those books looked in good condition."

"Oh, they were. I always look after my books, but I read them as well. A crease on the cover, worn corners, a cracked spine, a coffee stain— the sorts of things that happen to a loved book— reduce the price of any but the very rarest of books down to just a few dollars. I would guess that the copy of *Fer-de-Lance* might be worth fifty or sixty dollars at most. Sorry to burst your bubble."

"No problem," I force myself to say. "I'll go and tell Sam he was wrong." As I head back to my room, I think how I'm no closer to knowing if the entire adventure on Canoe Lake was completely planned or something much more complex and sinister. I guess I just have to accept what Grandfather told me—not all mysteries in real life have an answer.

ACKNOWLEDGMENTS

Thanks to Robin for suggesting that we all expand the series into the boys' earlier lives and to Eric, Shane, Ted, Richard, Norah and Sigmund for making the creation and marketing of the books such an eccentric yet delightful pleasure. Thanks also to Andrew for his continued faith in us all and his light editorial hand, to Vivian for her attention to detail and Teresa for another great cover.

JOHN WILSON is the author of more than forty books of fiction and nonfiction for kids, teens and adults. His work has won and been short-listed for many honors, including the Geoffrey Bilson, White Pine, Red Maple and Sheila Egoff awards. His novel about Henry Hudson's final voyage, *The Alchemist's Dream*, was a finalist for the Governor General's Award. John lives on Vancouver Island but tours across Canada presenting to kids of all ages in schools and at conferences. *The Missing Skull* is the prequel to *Lost Cause* in Seven (the series) and *Broken Arrow* in the The Seven Sequels. You can find out more about John, his books and his presentations on www.johnwilsonauthor.com.

THE SEVEN PREQUELS

HOW IT ALL BEGAN...
7 GRANDSONS
7 JOURNEYS
7 AUTHORS
7 ASTOUNDING PREQUELS

The seven grandsons from the bestselling **Seven (the series)** and **The Seven Sequels** return in **The Seven Prequels**, along with their daredevil grandfather, David McLean